THE gargoyle OVERHEAD

Philippa Dowding

Napoleon

Toronto, Ontario, Canada

Cover art and design by Emma Dolan

Le Conseil des Arts | The Canada Council
du Canada | for the Arts

We acknowledge the support of the Canada Council for the Arts for our publishing program. We acknowledge the financial support of the Government of Canada through the Book Publishing Industry Development Program (BPIDP) for our publishing activities.

Napoleon Publishing
an imprint of Napoleon & Company
Toronto, Ontario, Canada
www.napoleonandcompany.com

Printed in Canada

Mixed Sources
Product group from well-managed
forests, and other controlled sources
www.fsc.org Cert no. SW-COC-002358
© 1996 Forest Stewardship Council

14 13 12 11 10   5 4 3 2 1

Library and Archives Canada Cataloguing in Publication

Dowding, Philippa, date-
        The gargoyle overhead / Philippa Dowding.

ISBN 978-1-926607-03-0

        I. Title.

PS8607.O9874G38 2010   jC813'.6   C2010-900762-X

For Paul,
who knows Gargoth well

And for my father Marcus,
who knew him long ago

PROLOGUE

The year is 1664.

It is a beautiful, sunny day in a small churchyard in England. There are rolling green hills as far as the eye can see, beautiful old chestnut trees everywhere, and a very pretty little river running beside the church courtyard. It makes a sweet, soft sound as the water runs past the grassy banks. There is an ancient stone statue of a lion nearby, regally facing west on its pedestal of stone.

A boy is busy beside the little river, washing a basket of apples. He has just picked these apples from the abandoned orchard behind the church. No one else collects them but he and his father.

He is flicking flies away from his head. It is a hot day, and he would like to be back under a shady tree. He is dressed in breeches and a loose-fitting linen shirt. His golden hair is cropped very short, and he is barefoot.

As he is washing the apples, something hard hits the back of his head, and he turns quickly. In the grass beside him is an apple core, which he picks up and stares at, amazed. He looks around, but there is no one there.

This has happened before. In fact, it happens all the time, but just to him. His father never talks about being hit with flying apple cores, or about the strange sound the boy often hears when he is walking through the orchard. It is like the wind rustling in the winter leaves, or like a language he is just beginning to forget.

But he is wrong. It is neither of these things, which he is soon to find out.

Chapter One
Candles By Daye, at Night

Katherine stepped off the Queen streetcar and down into the hot Toronto evening. She hoisted her yellow canvas backpack a little higher and turned to whisper into it, "Gargoth, are you awake?"

She heard a familiar snap and growl and felt a small, hot body wriggle against her back. A sharp claw jabbed her hard in the ribs. Gargoth never did like waking up.

"Barga memi soth," a strange, growly voice said. But she heard it say, "Yes. I am now."

"Good," she snapped back. "We're here."

She walked past an old pub, with all the windows and doors open wide, and a tiny library. She never saw anyone at this tucked-away spot except old people and mothers with babies, but the library did have a nice roof garden with a goldfish pond and an ornamental crabapple tree.

Three stores over was her destination, Candles by Daye. It was an old, old storefront, bright red with a narrow green door. The front window was huge and overflowing with candles shaped like skulls and dragons, incense holders, healing chime balls, yoga and self-help books, crystals in every imaginable size and shape, and much more.

Katherine pushed hard on the old door, walked in, and locked it behind her. The air was heavily scented with cinnamon and years of burnt incense.

"Cassandra? Cassandra, we're here!" she shouted as she lowered the backpack to the floor. Gargoth hadn't felt that heavy when they'd started out, but by the time they'd crossed the city on the subway, then the streetcar, she felt like there were ten of him in the backpack.

He wriggled and complained a lot, too, which didn't help much.

"Up here! I'm up on the roof," came Cassandra Daye's voice from what seemed like miles away. Katherine bent down to her backpack and realized she'd forgotten to open it. There were muffled grunts coming from it, and the backpack wriggled and shook as though it contained a miniature tornado.

She opened it quickly, and Gargoth's leathery head popped out. He took a huge breath, as though he'd been suffocating for hours, and struggled out. Even if Katherine *had* wanted to help him, he wouldn't have let her, so she stood with her arms crossed, looking amused.

"Come on, she's upstairs," she said, heading toward the steep staircase at the back of the store.

Gargoth started after her, his heavy arms nearly touching the floor at his scaly feet, his leathery wings held tightly to his back, and a small pouch bulging at his side. At the bottom of the stairs, he looked up at the open door to the roof, the stars beyond twinkling and inviting. He sighed deeply. There were twenty steep

4

stairs to climb to get up to the rooftop, and Katherine had bounded up them in a few seconds.

He shook his wings for a few moments, and a look of concentration crossed his leathery face. His wings began to move, faster, faster, faster. He pushed his chin into the air as he worked his wings harder and harder, finally as hard as he could. His wings were fanning hard enough to blow dust across the floor of the store in little eddies and to gently move some of the closer crystals and bells hanging from the ceiling. They started softly ringing.

But nothing happened. He didn't budge. He sighed and stopped fanning his wings. He started to climb the steps slowly, mumbling about giants.

And if you have ever seen a gargoyle struggle up a steep set of stairs, you know it is not a pretty sight.

Chapter Two
Ambergine:
On Top of the World

The little gargoyle held on tight…

She was perched up high, as high as she had ever been, higher than she had ever wanted to be. It was late in the evening, and she had flown very hard to reach this place.

It was windy and frightening so high above the gigantic city. It sprawled below her like an enormous anthill, cars and trucks whizzing along in different directions on many, many roads and highways. Below her to the west was a huge, rounded sports stadium with a smooth white top. To the south, where the city ended, there was a dark, peaceful lake and a beautiful green island just offshore, with small twinkling lights on it. A boat was ferrying people back and forth between the city and the island.

I wish I was over there. It looks quiet at least, and not very windy, she thought just as a huge gust of wind threatened to blow her off her perch. She'd much rather be on the pretty green island than where she was, sitting dangerously on the top of a gigantic pointy building with a strange bulge near the top. She was balanced on the bulge. She couldn't even imagine what this building was for. She'd never seen anything like it. There were no people in it except for a few walking around in the bulgy bit below her. It was just tall, very tall, with flashing lights on the top. She'd picked this building because she knew it would be the best place to see the entire city splayed out beneath her. Once she got her bearings, she would leave this windy, dangerous spot for good (and the sooner the better).

She had to get to know this city called "Toronto", though, since she would be searching every corner of it until she found what she was looking for.

Chapter Three
Rooftop Pumpkins

Cassandra and Katherine were sitting on the rooftop in comfortable lawn chairs, sipping cool glasses of lemonade, deep in conversation. They tried to ignore the noises coming from the stairs as Gargoth climbed them, although they did exchange the odd worried look. Finally, he emerged through the small rooftop door. He stood for a while, glaring, his small chest heaving, and when neither Katherine nor Cassandra addressed him or seemed to notice him (they knew better), he stumped across the rooftop and flopped onto a small cushion.

Katherine and Cassandra were discussing soccer. Katherine was on a girl's soccer team, and they played all summer long. Cassandra had joined Katherine's parents, Hank and Marie Newberry, several times to cheer on Katherine and her teammates from the sidelines.

Occasionally, Gargoth also joined them, hidden in his yellow canvas backpack with eyeholes cut in the cloth. He was safely hidden but could still see the game around him. He wasn't entirely ready to admit it, but he was starting to enjoy watching the "ball-on-a-foot" game, as he called it.

"Well, that team last week was on steroids or something. Honestly, they were twice our size…" Katherine said.

Cassandra laughed. "I was tall at your age, almost six feet by then." Katherine looked awed.

"You were six feet by the time you were thirteen? You poor thing! I mean, not poor thing, but really, was there anyone else your height? I mean, any boys or anything?" Katherine looked down at her nail then bit it after the word "boys".

Cassandra laughed again. "A few, but they were too busy playing basketball to notice me."

Gargoth listened quietly. When he'd regained his breath, and his dignity, he left his cushion and waddled over to the lemonade pitcher. There was the cocoa mug which he had chosen from Cassandra's cupboard. It had an odd diamond-and-circle pattern on it like this:

■□■ ■□■ ■□■ ■□■ ■□■ ■□■

He poured himself a large mug of lemonade, downed it in one swig, then wiped his leathery mouth with the back of his claw.

"GARRPH," he gurgled (which is the noise a gargoyle makes when clearing its throat). "Lemmi lumina," he said. Katherine heard him say, "I need candles."

She was so surprised that Gargoth had spoken, she left her mouth open. They had visited Cassandra's rooftop several times since school ended, but in all those visits, this was the first time he had uttered a word.

His sudden request left her momentarily speechless. His rudeness didn't bother her; she was uscd to that.

9

"Candles? What for?"

Gargoth just glared at her, clearly not in the mood to answer any of her questions.

"Oh, never mind. Um, Cassandra, Gargoth would like to know if you have any candles…" she said.

"Candles? This is Candles by Daye, after all! Of course he can have candles. How many would he like?"

Cassandra loved Gargoth and adored everything to do with statues and gargoyles in particular, but try as she might, she had never been able to understand a word that he said. To her, his language always sounded like garbled whisperings, or like the wind rattling in the winter leaves.

Katherine on the other hand, understood every word (since most children can, and the occasional very wise adult). But understanding Gargoth was sometimes a mixed blessing, since he had a very short temper and tended to say things which would be better left unsaid. She turned to the little gargoyle. "Well? How many candles do you need?"

"One hundred and forty-eight," he answered in gargoyle, without hesitation.

She gasped. "One hundred and forty eight? You need one hundred and forty-eight candles? Why?"

She knew immediately that she had been too abrupt. Gargoth hated to be questioned. He turned from her, a heavy scowl on his face, staring off toward the dark city. The city skyline blazed in the distance, and tall office buildings shed thousands of bars of light over the dark houses and smaller buildings below. The CN Tower stood out majestically, a tall sentinel watching over the city.

Cassandra smiled. "Don't worry, Katherine. I have lots of candles. I just received three crates of Halloween candles—they're tiny orange pumpkins—and I only ordered one crate. I must have three hundred of those he can burn if he wants." She whisked away, and they heard her clomp back down the narrow stairs into her store.

Cassandra was not only very tall, she was also very clumsy. Katherine flinched when she heard a giant crash in the building below them: Cassandra had tripped or dropped something heavy.

"It's okay! I'm okay!" she yelled up to them as she tromped back upstairs. Gargoth hadn't moved from his cushion and just stared up at the stars.

Cassandra stomped heavily back onto the rooftop with a gigantic crate in her arms, out of breath and puffing hard, but looking very happy.

"Here, Gargoth! All the candles you could ever need. I hope you like orange-scented pumpkins!" She opened the crate and started pulling out tiny pumpkin candles. Gargoth hopped off his cushion and waddled over to the crate. He peered inside.

"They're smiling. They're smiling pumpkins. Why are they smiling?" he grumbled in his strange language. He looked up at Katherine, as though the boxful of happy, smiling pumpkins was somehow her fault.

"Does it matter?" she said. "You haven't told us what they're for yet. And Cassandra has very nicely donated them to you, without a second thought. You could just say 'Thank you Cassandra', without complaining."

Sometimes Katherine felt like she was teaching a rude little brother how to behave, except this little brother happened to be much, much older than her. Almost four hundred years older than her, in fact.

Gargoth mumbled something, which sounded very like "I hate pumpkins" and began carrying them in his leathery claws to an open part of the rooftop. He started to build a pile of tiny smiling orange pumpkin candles, oblivious to the girl and woman watching him.

"He says 'thank you, Cassandra'," Katherine lied.

Cassandra just smiled. She didn't care what Gargoth did. She didn't care that she didn't understand him. He was a living, breathing gargoyle, waddling around on her rooftop. He could have snarled and snapped at her every second of the day, and she wouldn't have minded.

Some people love dogs. Some people love small children. Some people can't get enough of bugs.

Cassandra Daye adored gargoyles, which, luckily for Gargoth, will one day soon save him from a terrible fate.

Chapter Four
Ambergine:
Among Hot Dog Eaters

The little gargoyle was tired…

She had flown all night, and she needed to sleep. Dawn was breaking over the city, and she wanted to be safely hidden before the sun rose. Lately, she had been sleeping among the statues of giant people at the big white sports stadium by the lake. The huge fibreglass figures were sort of like gargoyles, although none of them was alive (which was probably just as well, she decided, since they were all about ten metres tall).

Today she'd decided to sleep on the statue of a giant man with a hot dog stuffed in his mouth. "He doesn't look very appealing," she thought, "but I guess he'll do." Her small leathery wings carried her slowly off the roof of the dome (it was closed for the day), and let her settle awkwardly on the giant hot dog man's bronze head.

She waddled along the statue's head then nestled deep into the wall of the building, safely hidden. She pulled her wings close about her and let her head fall onto her little chest.

I wonder what a hot dog tastes like? she thought as she began to doze. Soon she was snoring quietly.

Well, as quietly as a gargoyle can snore, even a delicate lady gargoyle like her.

She was hidden completely from the street, safe for now. If anyone looked up at the giant statues, they wouldn't notice one small gargoyle tucked away among them, even if she was snoring. There was no one around anyway except for an old man wearing very thick glasses and a baggy brown jacket resting on a bench nearby, a white hat on his knee.

That night, Ambergine would continue her search.

Chapter Five
Master of the Candles

Gargoth and Katherine were back on Cassandra's roof a few days later, with the stars twinkling overhead and the city blazing off in the distance to the west. The lemonade pitcher and apples were laid out again. Katherine and Cassandra were relaxing comfortably in folding chairs, but Gargoth's cushion was empty.

He was working feverishly on his pile of unlit pumpkin candles, moving them around the roof, placing a single one here, then there. He would put one down, lean his head to one side, then move the candle again a few centimetres in a different direction. Sometimes he would lie down flat on the roof to line up the candles, or sometimes climb up the small chimney ladder (which made Katherine very nervous) to see his creation, all the while with his lit pipe clamped tightly in his leathery lips. He was concentrating very hard, not paying any attention to Katherine and Cassandra at all. It was almost like they weren't there.

Although they knew better than to ask, Katherine and Cassandra were very curious about what he was doing. Was it a piece of art? Was it some ancient game? By now the candles were covering the entire roof in some sort of sequence, but it didn't make any sense to them. Since Cassandra had provided the candles, Gargoth hadn't said another word. He just went about his mysterious business, so until he decided to tell them what he was doing, they would just have to wait to find out.

Instead they were talking about soccer camp. "They play soccer all day, then swim all afternoon at the university pool. It sounds hard, but it's really fun. Two professional soccer players are running the camp this year, and we get to play an exhibition game on their field. A professional field, Cassandra!"

Cassandra smiled. Katherine sighed. "I might not be able to go, though. Mom and Dad have to go to my mom's cousin's daughter's wedding in Saskatoon or something. I've been begging them to let me stay home, but they won't let me stay alone. Also, we aren't sure what to do with…" she hesitated and glanced over at Gargoth.

Since he was a good way across the roof, she dropped her voice to a whisper and said, "We aren't sure what to do with Gargoth for an entire week, though. He knows we're leaving, and I don't think he's all that happy about it..."

The week before, her mother had told him they were leaving for a holiday. He'd stormed into the bushes at the back of their little yard and wouldn't come out for hours. He'd sulked and pouted and wouldn't even stroke their calico cat Milly (and they were great friends). And he hadn't talked to her mother since.

It was a little awkward. They couldn't take him away for a whole week. He *was* a gargoyle, not a pet, after all. Even if they were used to him walking and talking and being very much alive in their backyard, Katherine doubted that the nice people at the wedding would be all that okay with it. Besides, Gargoth was terrible in the car. They'd only tried that once, and it hadn't gone at all well. She couldn't begin to imagine what he would be like in an airplane.

"So, I'm going to miss the best soccer camp ever, and we're kind of stuck about Gargoth…" Katherine finished.

They looked over at the gargoyle, who was deep in thought, struggling with an armload of smiling pumpkins. The crate was half empty, he had used so many.

Cassandra put down her knitting. "You know, you could both stay here for the week. Gargoth could stay up here on the roof, doing whatever it is he's doing with the candles. And I have an extra bedroom in my apartment downstairs for you."

Katherine gasped. "Do you think so, Cassandra? That would be *so* great. We'd have to ask Mom and Dad…it might not be so easy to convince them…"

Just at that moment, Gargoth waddled over and stood before them with a single smiling pumpkin candle in his claw. He turned it over and lit it with the coals in the stump of his pipe.

"I'm finished," he said. "Could you help me set my beacon ablaze?"

Chapter Six
Gargoth's Beacon

Katherine had a confused look on her face. "Beacon? What do you mean? Do you want us to help you light the candles, Gargoth?"

"Yes, Katherine. Here," he handed her the candle. He offered Cassandra another lit candle.

"The three of us can light them quickly together," he said. Katherine nodded and began lighting candles. "He wants us to help him light them all," she translated for Cassandra, who followed along, a little confused but happy to help out.

For the next several minutes, the three of them went from candle to candle, lighting smiling pumpkins. With his clumsy, leathery claws, Gargoth found it hard to light the candles easily and kept scorching himself.

THIS IS VERY IMPORTANT: try to avoid the scent of scorched gargoyle, if you ever happen across it. It's a little like overcooked cabbage and cat-box, with a dash of moldering dead rat thrown in for good measure. Pretty much the exact opposite of anything nice you've ever smelled in your life. Both Cassandra and Katherine tried to hide the fact that they were holding their noses, which made lighting the candles very difficult. Gargoth didn't seem to notice.

It took them ages, but despite the horrible stench of burnt gargoyle and the fact that the candles were hard to light, they did finally get them all lit.

Eventually Cassandra's rooftop was alight with one hundred and forty-eight shimmering orange-scented pumpkin candles (which strangely did little to mask the stink of burned gargoyle flesh). They looked very pretty glowing softly in the dark night, but the reason for their arrangement was still a mystery to Katherine and Cassandra.

Gargoth climbed back up the ladder on the chimney to see the candles better. He climbed down and waddled to a few candles, moving them slightly. He returned to the chimney to look again. Eventually he flopped onto his small cushion beside the lemonade pitcher.

He poured himself a long drink, refilled his pipe, then wiggled comfortably on his cushion, blowing smoke rings toward the stars.

Eventually Katherine couldn't stand it any longer. She looked over at Cassandra, who was knitting again, and who could only shrug.

Katherine had enough. "Okay Gargoth, what's going on?" she asked. "What's this 'beacon' for?"

He propped himself up on one elbow and sighed. "We have to be patient, Katherine. It may take a long while, but my beacon may bring the one I wish to summon."

"Which one? Who do you wish to summon? What are you talking about?" Katherine was demanding again, which was never good with Gargoth. If you got too snoopy, or too direct, he'd stop talking altogether, which was very annoying, since it usually only happened when you were excited. And you were probably excited because something interesting was about to happen, which hardly seemed fair.

Gargoth blew out a long stream of smoke. "You're overexcited, Katherine," he said quietly. "Be calm, child."

Katherine frowned and turned to Cassandra. "He's teasing me. He says his 'beacon' may bring the one he wishes to summon, whatever that means…" She stopped in mid-sentence.

Then she knew. The other gargoyle. The one who had flown away from Cassandra's shop just days before she and Gargoth had entered it last spring.

"Do you mean the lost gargoyle?" she asked quietly.

"Yes," he said simply. "It is a beacon for my greatest friend, the only one who can help me, the gargoyle Ambergine."

Chapter Seven
Ambergine:
Among Angels

The little gargoyle was perched up high, looking over the dark water…

The moon was setting and reflected off the surface of the lake in shiny splashes. She could see waves and boats at anchor in the harbour nearby. Her search in the backyards, churches and parks near the giant hot dog eater had failed. She'd spent the last few days sleeping hidden in the wings of an angel over a great arched gate. Many busy roads met at the angel's feet far below. She'd overheard someone call this place "The Prince's Gates". It opened onto a wide open space with a long building and horses inside.

Below her, the city streets were still—it was five a.m., after all. There was no one around except an old beggar with a baggy brown jacket and a white straw hat, a pair of thick glasses on the ground beside him, sleeping under a tree. Even a big city is still sometimes. She knew that soon the great red locomotion machines would start rolling by her, then she would have to hide for the day once again.

"Perhaps tonight…" she whispered as she dozed against the great angel. "If you grant me one wish, sweet angel, please let me find him tonight…"

With that simple prayer, Ambergine fell fast asleep.

Chapter Eight
Mark of the Stonemason

A few nights later, Katherine was standing at the bottom of the stairs to Cassandra's rooftop once again. Without saying it out loud, Katherine and Gargoth had reached an agreement about the stairs: Katherine now carried Gargoth up in the backpack. He didn't get out or even let on that they had arrived at the store until they reached the rooftop.

Cassandra greeted them happily at the top of the stairs, standing amid a blaze of one hundred and forty-eight flaming orange-scented pumpkin candles.

"Hi, Katherine! Hi, Gargoth!" she said. "I lit your beacon." She exchanged a glance with Katherine.

"Thanks, Cassandra," Katherine breathed, very relieved that she and Cassandra would be spared any more exposure to the delights of scorched gargoyle flesh.

Gargoth climbed out of the backpack, waddled across the rooftop, and flopped onto the soft cushion. He looked dejected.

"What's the matter?" Katherine stood over him with her arms crossed. She was so used to his moods, she barely even noticed them any more.

He was silent for a while. As usual, he wasn't going to be rushed into anything. He pulled out his pipe and lit it, then slowly wriggled himself into a comfortable position on the cushion, blowing puffs of smoke up into the night. A streetcar rumbled loudly as it passed by far below them. A police siren wailed somewhere nearby.

Katherine sighed and went to sit beside Cassandra, who was knitting something that looked kind of like a giant green scarf. Being a giantess (or something pretty close), Cassandra had huge hands, and knitting wasn't all that easy for her. But she never gave up, even if she maybe should have.

Katherine was about to say something when Gargoth cleared his throat. "I would tell you the beginning of a long story tonight, I think. But I fear it will be difficult for our friend Cassandra to follow along," he said.

"I'll translate for her, don't worry," Katherine answered. "It's okay. Are you finally going to tell us what the candles are for?"

"Yes, Katherine. That and more. But first I must tell you that I fear the beacon will fail. It has taken me a long time to regain any hope…" He paused, struggling for the right words, then continued. "I think she has gone. I think Ambergine has abandoned me and will never see the beacon, and I will be forsaken here forever."

Katherine felt a jab of sadness, hearing the longing in Gargoth's voice. It was very rare for him to be so open with her. "Maybe if you tell us the story you want to tell, it will make waiting easier," she said. "I really want to hear whatever it is you have to tell us."

It was true. She really did want to hear. Gargoth was

nothing if not interesting. His stories were always worth the wait.

"But first, please tell us one thing right now: what is the beacon? *How* is it a beacon?" she said, sounding a little desperate.

Gargoth sighed again. "Humans are so impatient!" he said, shaking his head. "Okay, Katherine. Go and climb up the chimney at the edge of the roof and look down upon the lit candles. I think you will see then."

Obediently, she got up and tiptoed through the lit candles across the roof. As she laid her hand on the short ladder attached to the chimney, Cassandra looked up in alarm.

"What are you doing?" she asked.

"He wants me to look at the pattern of the beacon."

"Be careful! Your parents won't be happy with me if you get hurt."

"I'll just be a second," Katherine answered.

She climbed the rungs of the ladder and leaned against the old chimney, looking down over the rooftop of brightly lit candles. There was a pattern, but it didn't mean much to her.

"What do you see?" Gargoth asked from his cushion.

"Well, I see two diamonds on top of each other, inside a giant circle, I think. It's kind of hard to tell for sure…" she finished.

"Excellent, Katherine," Gargoth said.

She climbed down from the chimney ladder and brushed red chimney brick dust off her hands and shorts. She carefully navigated through the candles back to her lawn chair.

"Okay, but what is it?"

Gargoth slowly got to his feet and waddled over to his friends. He turned his back on them and opened his little wings wide. "See there, between my wings, is there a mark?" he asked.

Katherine moved in closely to see what he meant. She held her head close to the little gargoyle's back (but didn't breathe in too deeply, Gargoth's burnt flesh smell still lingered about him). Then she saw it: a small mark about the size of a coin, right between his shoulders, slightly closer to his right wing.

It was two diamonds one on top of the other, inside a circle, like this:

"I see it, Gargoth. But what is it?"

"It is my beacon, Katherine. It is also the mark of my creator, the stonemason who made me. He carved one on every statue that he made. But in the whole world there are only two living gargoyles who carry this mark, as far as I know. I have one…and Ambergine has the other."

Chapter Nine
Ambergine:
Among University Students

The little gargoyle shook her wings...

They were heavy and tired. She huddled deep into the marble wall behind the soldier from a long-ago war. She was looking out over another busy street, but far from the water now. She had looked for days in the houses and backyards and gardens around the angel but found nothing. The statues she had found to hide her this time were in the middle of a large university. It was a group of soldiers and angels, some with wings like hers, or with guns or swords. She liked the students walking below her: they all looked busy and had much to say.

Tonight she was going to search along the road called Queen Street, where she knew there was a store called the Golden Nautilus. She had already seen it from overhead, and it looked like the kind of place that had gargoyles.

She yawned. She would have to get ready to fly soon. Night was coming.

If Ambergine had peeked out from her hiding place,

she might have noticed an old man standing at the foot of the soldier statue she was hiding in. But it's just as well that she didn't.

He was wearing thick glasses, a white straw hat, and a big baggy brown jacket. He was looking straight up, right at her hiding spot, as if he were waiting for something. The setting sun shining right into his eyes didn't seem to bother him one bit.

Chapter Ten
The Story Begins

The candles blazed.

Katherine and Cassandra were seated on their lawn chairs, Gargoth was on his cushion looking up at the sky. "Are you ready then?" he asked.

"Yep. Are you ready for Gargoth's story, Cassandra?" Katherine asked.

Cassandra didn't even look up from her knitting. "Yes!"

"Here it is then, a long story, about a time long ago," Gargoth said. And with that simple introduction, he began. "As you know Katherine, I was created in England in 1604. I was made by a master stonemason, a Frenchman. He travelled far and wide through villages and towns, using his skill to make beautiful statues, or to add elegant finishing touches to buildings of stone. His name was Tallus…"

"Oh! That's why you're Gargoth of Tallus!" Katherine exclaimed.

Gargoth shot her a dark look and said, "That's correct. Now quiet please, Katherine. This is a long story, and we'll never get through it if you interrupt me.

"I believe I may have been his final creation. No one ever heard of the master French stonemason Tallus after 1604.

"The little churchyard where I was created was a beautiful place. There was once a brotherhood of monks who lived in the church, and they planted an apple orchard and many beautiful flowers and bushes, but the brothers were all gone by the time I arrived. King Henry VIII didn't like monasteries and had shut them all down years before."

"Why?" Katherine asked.

Gargoth shot her another dark look and sighed. "Look, if I go into all the ins-and-outs of English history, we'll never leave this rooftop. Look it up—it was called the Dissolution of the Monasteries. That 'net' on the box you like should be able to tell you about it." Katherine knew that Gargoth was referring to the Internet and her computer. She made a mental note to learn more about King Henry VIII.

Gargoth took a few puffs of his pipe. "It was a lovely place, but I was completely alone. There was another statue in the churchyard, an ancient stone lion, but I hated it. It wasn't alive like me, just a lump of cold stone. How I would rage at it! How I wished it were alive, just to have someone to talk to. It reminded me, every day, of how lonely I was.

"I was alone for years, decades. England went through a terrible civil war, and still I hid in the church tower, all alone.

"Then one day, a young boy arrived in the church-yard. He came with his father to pick the apples in the old

29

orchard: people were starving in England at that time and had to eat whatever they could find. They came year after year. Winter would come, and I wouldn't see him again until late the next summer. Finally, when he was almost a man, I decided I would speak to him.

"His name was Philip, and he was the first friend I ever had."

Gargoth's Story, 1664
The Empty Basket

The boy reached gingerly into the grass and picked up the half-eaten apple core. He left the basket of apples he was collecting at the bottom of the apple tree and walked toward the church.

"That's the third time this week," he said to himself. "Whoever is doing this is a really good shot." As if to remind himself of this fact, he rubbed the back of his head where the apple core had just hit him.

He brushed off his breeches. He looked carefully up into the church tower, still holding the apple core. He raised his hand to shade his eyes from the glare of the setting sun.

"HULLOO," he finally shouted. "I know you're up there. There are plenty of apples for everyone; you don't have to throw them at me."

He waited and listened, but there was no answer. So he tried again.

"HELLO! Whoever you are, you'd better come out now and give yourself up. I know you've been throwing apples at me when I'm out here in the orchard."

ZING! An apple core whizzed right at him. He ducked behind a tree just in time to hear it smack the other side, hard. He stuck his head out from behind the tree, and shouted, "STOP IT! What are you doing?"

At that moment, he saw the basket of apples he had just picked disappear behind a tree. He jumped up to run toward it but quickly had to take cover.

Someone was throwing the entire basket of apples at him! Each time he stuck his head out, trying to catch a glimpse of the culprit, an apple whizzed by, sending him ducking for cover.

ZING! ZING! ZING! A torrent of apples flew at him. The entire apple orchard was ringing with the sound of apples smashing against the trees.

His heart was starting to pound. Who was doing this? Who was wasting an entire basket of apples throwing them at him, and why?

And who was such a good shot?

Suddenly the apples stopped flying, and the boy heard someone calling him. It was his father.

"Philip! Philip, where are you? The cart is loaded, we're ready to go! Where are you hiding, boy?"

Philip stood up and peered around the side of the tree. "Here, Father! I'm over here in the orchard." He moved away from the tree and ran toward the spot where he had left his apple basket. He and his father reached the basket at the same moment.

It was empty and lying on its side. A few trampled apples lay nearby.

"What happened here?" his father asked, concerned.

"I…I really don't know, Father," Philip stammered.

"Well, where are the apples?" His father crossed his arms, never a good sign.

"I...I don't know. They're everywhere. They're all over the orchard, Father," he said, confused and upset.

His father looked around. He saw apples everywhere, smashed against the trees, and many piled up and ruined at the bottom of one particular tree. He gave Philip a hard stare. "If you're going to do target practice, Philip, please use the river stones and not food for our table. Every apple you've wasted here could have been saved and dried for food in the winter ahead. You will have extra chores to do tonight."

His father never really got angry, but Philip could tell he was displeased as he marched back toward the waiting horse and cart beside the old church gate.

There would be no apples for lunch tomorrow. There would be fewer dried apples for the winter ahead.

As Philip bent down to retrieve the empty apple basket and follow his father to their old cart, he heard the most amazing sound.

It was like a creaky cartwheel groaning uphill under a great weight. Or maybe, just maybe, someone high up in the church tower was laughing.

Gargoth's Story, 1664
The Lion Roars

It was getting dark. Philip wasn't really sure he wanted to be there, but despite his complaints, his father had insisted. Since the incident the week before, when an entire basket of apples had been destroyed, Philip had been trying to avoid the churchyard altogether.

The more he thought about it, the more sure he was. Someone *had* been laughing at him from the church tower that day. The sound was odd, though, not like a laugh he'd ever heard before. It was chilling and whispery and kind of sad. It left him thinking of spirits. Philip was a very sensible and brave twelve-year-old boy, however, and he was pretty sure that spirits couldn't pelt you with apple cores. At least, not so accurately.

Still. Someone *was* up there, hiding in the church tower, he was sure of that now, which made his current task all the more unpleasant. He had been sent to the abandoned apple orchard to pick a small sack of apples for a sick neighbour, even as the sun was setting.

He wasn't going to tell his father that he was too afraid to go. His home wasn't far away, though, and he was quick on his feet. He could outrun almost anyone who tried to catch him.

He kept telling himself this as he unlatched the creaky wooden churchyard gate and slowly swung it open. It made a very loud screech which Philip hadn't noticed by day.

"Why is everything louder at dusk?" he asked himself, trying to seem casual. The sun was low in the western sky, sending a beautiful orange glow through the small churchyard. The ancient stones still held the warmth of the sun. The only sound was the little river babbling quietly. He stood beside the river for a moment and looked around.

Philip breathed out. "It's not so bad," he thought. He hoisted his small sack and turned toward the apple orchard. He stopped dead in his tracks and gasped.

The ancient stone lion statue was broken! The lion's left ear was broken off and lay jagged and smashed in the grass at its feet.

Philip stared. The lion was the only statue in the village. It had stood in the middle of the churchyard for as long as anyone could remember, proud and fierce on its pedestal of stone. It wasn't a large statue, but it was very regal.

"Who would do this?" he wondered, dragging his shirt sleeve across his stinging eyes. He was sure the lion statue had not been broken the previous week when he and his father had last been there.

He moved toward the broken piece of statue lying in the grass but stopped suddenly. Something had moved in the apple orchard just a few feet away. He stood stock still, barely breathing. His heart started knocking in his chest. He knew someone was behind him.

"Who…" he cleared his dry throat, "who's there?" he tried to shout. He wanted to sound brave and big, but unfortunately his voice chose that very moment to break. He sounded like a frightened child, which is exactly what he was.

There was nothing but silence. Philip turned slowly, too afraid to run, and couldn't believe his eyes.

A basket overflowing with apples waited beside the orchard. He couldn't tell why, but somehow he knew they were for him.

He gripped his apple sack tightly and slowly approached the basket. He jumped across the little river, and in ten strides stood at the edge of the orchard with the overflowing apple basket at his feet. The sun was just about to dip behind the nearby hills for the night.

Philip took a deep breath. "Who is here?" he asked quietly.

Nothing moved, not a bird, not a branch, and even the tiny river seemed momentarily silent. So he took another deep breath, and asked again, slightly louder this time. "Who are you? You might as well come out. I know you're here."

But nothing could have prepared him for what happened next.

A small, squat creature with leathery wings stepped out from behind the tree at his feet and looked up into Philip's face. Philip wasn't absolutely sure, but there might have been tears in the creature's eyes.

"Hamithin sorken behem. Sorth belamont," was

what the creature said.

But Philip heard it say in its strange whispery voice, "Do not be afraid. I am alone."

Gargoth's Story, 1664
Smoke Rings
in the Orchard

Philip stood completely still, barely daring to breathe. The sack for collecting apples had fallen, forgotten, from his hand into the grass. His face held a strange look of bewilderment and dawning comprehension.

The creature was hunched at his feet, looking at the ground. Eventually Philip was sure the creature was crying, since he heard the *plunk plunk* of its tears hitting the earth and saw small columns of steam rise from where they fell.

Philip clenched and unclenched his fists, understanding now that he was in no immediate danger. He cleared his throat. "What is that language you speak? It is strange and whispery and not my tongue, I think, and yet I understand you."

The creature shrugged. "Vox a voxi. Toth audi. Horsa?" it said. Philip heard it say, "I speak as I speak. You hear as you hear. What does it matter?"

They looked at each other, silent. Philip realized he would have to be content with that answer, such as it was.

"Well, where did you learn to throw apples like that?" he asked. It was all he could think of. He wasn't sure what else to say. What *do* you say to a bizarre creature like this, anyway? Philip wasn't even entirely sure what the creature was. He didn't want to appear foolish—perhaps this was a new kind of farm animal recently imported to England? One he'd never heard of, an odd one to be sure. A creature crossed between a small dog and a large bird? Perhaps in the New World, animals spoke like this one? Whatever it was, it clearly wasn't going to hurt him, not at the moment anyway.

The creature looked up at him, then used a claw (it looked *very* sharp) to wipe away the tears coursing down its cheeks.

"Belo grathen memimi," it said miserably, but Philip heard it say, "I practice a lot."

Philip considered this. "Did you break the ancient stone lion in the churchyard?" he asked gruffly. Now that he was no longer so afraid, he felt he could ask a pointed question.

He was surprised by the angry answer from the creature (but I'm just going to translate it here, or we'll be here all day): "Yes! I broke it! It has tormented me for too long! I hate it!" With this the creature snapped and growled and turned to look at the broken lion statue across the small river. "It deserved to be broken!" As if to make the point again, the creature picked up a stone at its feet and threw it at the lion. It glanced off the lion's tail, falling harmlessly into the grass.

Philip took a step back, wary of the creature's sudden burst of anger. It seemed quite capable of hurting him now; its teeth and claws were very sharp, regardless of its small size.

"Why?" Philip demanded, angry himself now. "Stupid creature! You know that the villagers are going to think that I did it. My father already thinks that I wasted an entire basket of apples in target practice last week when it was really you…" He stopped. "Why *have* you been throwing apples at me, anyway?"

The creature sighed. It stayed silent as it stuck a claw into a pouch at its side and pulled out a briarwood pipe and some cured tobacco. With a tinder-pistol (a very old kind of lighter), it struck a spark onto the pipe and lit it. Strong smoke curled up about its head and caught in Philip's nose. He sneezed.

"Well?" Philip said, squinting as his eyes watered, determined to get an answer. "Why?"

The little pipe-smoker leaned against a tree and blew smoke rings up about its head, eyeing the boy. Philip had never seen anyone (or anything) smoke before, although his father had told him about the new phenomenon. His father had seen a merchant smoking in a nearby village when delivering a carthorse for auction. The wealthy nobles and the people from the great town of London were known to particularly like the curious native plant from across the ocean. But no one in his little village smoked, at least none he knew of. Now that he was so close to it for the first time, he decided it was a strange custom. It smelled awful and burned his eyes and nose. And it made him cough.

The creature spoke again. "Why did I throw apples at you? Because I wanted you to know I was here. And the river stones would have hurt you—see what they did to the lion."

Philip, who was suddenly very thankful that he hadn't been collecting river stones in the basket the week before, wanted to ask many questions. He wanted to know exactly what the creature was, and how it had come to be in the churchyard. Why did it hate the stone lion?

And most of all, why did it want Philip to know it was there? As far as Philip was concerned, he would have been just as happy if he'd remained ignorant of that fact.

Just as he was going to ask one of the many questions on the tip of his tongue, a voice rang out from the church gate.

"Philip? Philip? Where are you?" It was his father. Philip suddenly realized that it was quite dark. The sun had gone down completely. In his conversation with the creature, he hadn't noticed.

"I have to go!" Philip said urgently.

But the creature was already filling Philip's forgotten sack with apples from the surrounding trees. "Here, take these, and the basket. Be quick," it said. Then it vanished into the apple orchard, right before Philip's eyes.

But not before Philip heard the whispery voice say, "My name is Gargoth of Tallus. Come again soon, and I will answer all your questions."

Chapter Eleven
More from the Rooftop

The candles were burning low. Katherine was telling Cassandra everything that Gargoth had told her. Gargoth stood up for a while and walked through the candles, checking that they were all still lit. He took a drink of lemonade and ate a few apples. He was forbidden to throw the apple cores off the roof (there were people walking by on the street down below), but he did do a little target practice with the ladder on the chimney. He was still an excellent shot.

When he had rested from his storytelling and Katherine had translated the story for Cassandra, he took up his spot on the cushion, lit his pipe once again, and continued.

"Philip and I became great friends. After the shock of our first meeting, he returned to the churchyard as often as he could. We met in the autumn of 1664, and all through that winter, he came to talk to me again and again. I had never had a friend, so there was much for him to teach me. He didn't, for instance, like being pelted with apple cores. Nor did he like it when I stuck my tongue out at him, or threw river stones better than he did in target practice. He did, however, like to tell me about his world outside the churchyard, and about his father, mother and sister.

"Soon, though, he began to tell me stories of a different kind. There was a great plague crossing the country. In the towns and villages people were dying, sometimes leaving entire villages empty, but for a lucky few. In the city of London, hundreds of people were dying each day. Philip came to the churchyard one day to tell me that the plague was in his village, and he didn't know when he would see me again. Many weeks, then months went by, and I was alone.

"One summer night, I heard the churchyard gate creak open, and someone calling me. Philip had come. But disaster had come too: while he was away with the sheep in the fields, many villagers had died of plague, including his father, mother and sister. He was an orphan, all alone in the world. I was his only friend.

"He sat mute by the river of the churchyard for many weeks, alone except for me. I tried to encourage him with stories and antics and target practice, and eventually, he did rise from the riverbank and speak once more. Philip's father had told him of an uncle who lived in a small village in France. Philip was going to France, and I was going with him.

"One autumn day, we left the only home either of us had ever known. Before we left, I tried my best to fix the stone lion, but it was no use. His broken ear lies in the long grass at his feet even now, no doubt." Gargoth grew thoughtful.

"How did you get to France?" Katherine asked, forgetting

about the not-interrupting-or-this-was-going-to-take-forever rule.

Gargoth frowned. "First by horse and cart, then by boat, then on foot. It was a long and difficult journey." He drew his wings tightly about him. "And I didn't like it one bit."

Gargoth's Story, 1665
Cart and Boat

It was raining again. Gargoth was huddled deep inside an apple sack and was being jarred mercilessly against the baskets of apples all around him. They had hit upon the clever idea of hiding Gargoth in a sack so Philip could carry him about safely hidden. They had even cut eyeholes into the cloth so Gargoth could see a little of what was happening around them.

But he didn't really like it. And it was far from dry or comfortable. He was tucked behind Philip, who was driving the horse and cart. Despite his best efforts to keep dry, Gargoth was wet and grouchy. It was raining so hard, he couldn't even light his pipe.

"That at least would be some small comfort," he muttered, clutching his dripping wings tightly to himself.

"I hope you're not thinking about your pipe again, Gargoth?" Philip said from the front seat. "I for one am very glad that you can't light the foul stuff. I can breathe fresh air once again!" he added with a chuckle.

At that moment mud splashed up into the cart and drenched them from below, almost as much as they were being drenched by rain from above.

"Was there ever such a muddy country as England?" Gargoth growled, flattening his ears against his head.

"France is muddier, I hear," Philip said, laughing. "That'll make you happy, won't it, Gargoth?"

Gargoth stuck his tongue out at Philip's back but didn't answer.

The little horse was plodding very slowly along a dark country lane. Because they only travelled at night, Gargoth and Philip had seen almost no one since they'd set out on their journey, many nights before. Their store of apples was getting low, and Gargoth was sick of the bumpy cart ride. Try as he might, there was no way to avoid being bumped and jostled as the cart travelled south along the paths and open meadows of England.

But he knew the journey was almost over, for the next day would take them to their destination: the town of Dover.

As dawn was nearing, they found an old barn to sleep in. It was abandoned and was falling into disrepair, but the two travellers didn't mind. It was dry and less muddy than the road. They watered and brushed the little horse, leaving her in an empty stall of hay, then made their own meal of dried apples and water. As the sky was just beginning to turn pink in the east, they curled up in the dry haystack of the barn, listening to the lonely hooting of owls as they fell asleep.

Many hours later, they woke to a bright and sunny afternoon. The weather had changed, and the wind had shifted to the south. As Gargoth roused himself and began gathering sticks for a brief fire, his nose caught the fresh scent of something he did not recognize. The air had a funny tang to it, a bitter taste he couldn't name.

As Philip rose and stretched and joined him, plucking loose hay from his blonde hair, he sniffed the air as well.

"What is that on the air, do you think?" he asked.

Gargoth struck his tinder-pistol against some bracken he had collected and blew gently on the spark. The little fire caught. He placed a clawful of sticks over the growing fire and pushed back on his haunches. "I cannot say. It smells like autumn nights when it has rained and rained and washed everything clean. But there is something else."

The two travellers had to put their puzzlement aside and ready themselves for the final hours of their weary journey. As the afternoon drew on, they ate a few apples, laced the little horse into the harness and set off to Dover.

As their horse and cart turned off the cart path, to a larger, sturdier lane, then to a larger road, then to a busy thoroughfare through the noisy town, the scent they could not place grew and grew, until they both understood what it was: the ocean! They could smell salt water.

They had both heard of the ocean, but neither had ever seen it, nor could really imagine that much water, which looked as though it never ended.

The smell of the ocean burned Gargoth's nose as he strained to see the town through the eyeholes of his sack. He couldn't see much, but what he did see filled him with amazement: many people, busy taverns, horses and carts, endless water, a shoreline of tall white cliffs, and strange birds wheeling and crying in the air above him.

And what looked like carts floating in the water. He had to ask Philip what the things in the water were, since he had no name for them.

"They're called boats, Gargoth. Now shhh," Philip whispered over his shoulder into the sack behind him. Gargoth could just make out many, many wooden boats, some with tall wooden sticks in the middle and great white cloths hanging on them, flapping in the breeze. Others were much smaller, with small sticks on the sides.

Gargoth could only stare. He had to be quiet in case someone discovered him hiding in the sack, so he hung silently over Philip's shoulder through all the events of that long, strange night. They arrived in the town just as the villagers were setting their fires for the evening meal, and Gargoth choked on the heavy smoke which hung in the streets.

The first thing Philip did was to climb down from the cart and carefully lead the horse through the muddy town to a sign hanging over a doorway. The sign had a horse and cart on it. He knocked hard, and the top part of the wooden door swung outward immediately.

"Yes?" came a gruff voice.

"How much for this horse and cart? My father has sent me to sell it." Gargoth couldn't see what was happening very well, but he couldn't believe his ears. Philip hadn't mentioned this before.

Gargoth heard the bottom part of the door swing open and caught sight of a huge beard as a giant man walked past his sack, around the cart. He could hear the man breathing hard. He sensed that the man was running his hands over the horse's back and hooves and over her head and nose. Then he heard the man turn toward the cart and bang his hands on the wood, giving it a good shake.

"Where's your father then, boy?" he heard the gruff voice say.

"He's back in the village with my young sister and mother," Philip answered.

It wasn't a lie, exactly. His father *was* with Philip's mother and sister, buried deep in the village field.

"This isn't much of a horse, more an oversized pony," the man grunted again.

"She's sturdy though, sir, and good-tempered. She's not seen more than four summers altogether. She'll last her new owner many years. She's never foaled, but her mother had many good healthy foals." Philip said all this very quickly but stoutly. Gargoth knew his friend well enough to catch the odd tone in his voice; Philip was not much of a liar.

There was a long pause, then Gargoth heard the man go back into the doorway, followed by the jingle of coins. He counted some of them out into Philip's hand then said, "Go quickly, before I ask any more questions."

Philip stuffed the coins into his linen shirt, then reached into the cart and hoisted Gargoth's sack onto his back. Another sack he filled with the remaining apples in the back of the cart, then he turned away from his father's horse and cart without another word and headed toward the water's edge.

He couldn't bear to run his hand over the horse's

soft nose even one more time. He was trying hard not to remember the morning she was born, and how he and his father had leaned over the fence of the farmyard, watching as the newborn foal took her first steps into the world.

He walked very quickly down to the waterfront, drawing his shirt sleeve over his burning eyes only once.

When it grew quiet and there were fewer people nearby, Gargoth spoke up. "Why did you do that? Why did you sell your father's horse and cart?" he growled angrily.

"How do you think we are going to get across the English Channel? Can you swim? I can't," Philip snapped back, nasty for the first and only time in their long friendship.

Gargoth was silent and scowled deep in his sack. He didn't even complain when he realized that Philip was going to use the coins to buy their way on a *boat* to cross the huge expanse of water before them.

He stayed silent when later that night Philip rested him on the floor of a busy tavern, and he was kicked and jostled by dozens of large muddy boots. Loud men and women sat at the long wooden table around Philip, eating mutton stew noisily and sloppily from huge wooden bowls. Gargoth did not complain when he was bumped and banged on Philip's back to a damp spot near the water where Philip fell asleep in the sand, snoring gently. Great white cliffs rose at their backs into the night sky, and the enormous ocean spanned before them. Gargoth did not sleep at all that night but kept watch over his friend, hunched and peering out over the dark beach and the even darker, endless water.

But Gargoth could not keep silent the next day. He woke to Philip shouldering his sack and saying, "Off to the *Merryman*, Gargoth. Our ship is waiting. She will be sailing with the early tide."

"The *Merryman*? Do you mean that tiny speck of wood we saw yesterday? We are sailing the ocean on *that*?" Gargoth could not contain his panic.

Philip laughed. "Yes, my sturdy gargoyle. We are shipping out on *that*."

Gargoth trembled. He was going to cross the English Channel in the smallest boat they had seen. And he didn't like the captain one bit, or the way he kept asking Philip to show him what was in his apple sack.

"Apples, what do you think?" Philip finally said, angry with the man. The captain had looked at him oddly then but left the sack alone.

"When are we leaving?" Gargoth managed to ask.

"Now," Philip answered casually, biting deeply into an apple. He ignored the coughing and spluttering from the sack over his shoulder and strode out onto the little wooden pier. Gargoth could hear his boots striking the wood as he walked.

It was a beautiful, clear day. The birds overhead (which Gargoth had learned were called "seagulls") wheeled and cried, and the breeze was fine and fair. The water between England and France was calm, still and very blue. There wasn't a wave on the water or a cloud in the sky. As Philip stood upon the deck of the vessel which would take him away from England forever, he barely looked back. He shook the captain's hand, and after a few more travellers had joined them (including one very big lady with a basket of geese that never stopped gabbling), he took his place on the deck, watching for France. It would take them not more than twenty hours to sail to the shore of their new home, if the weather stayed fair.

And all the while, he ignored the snorting, sneezing, grunting sound from the sack over his shoulder. He was quite sure that most people would think the sound was coming from the big lady and her noisy geese.

Chapter Twelve
More Night at Daye's

Two nights later, Katherine and Gargoth were back at Cassandra's. The roof was ablaze with lit pumpkin candles. Gargoth was loudly eating an apple. Cassandra was working on her knitting, while Katherine was talking to them both.

"So, it's settled then, Gargoth. You and I come back tomorrow to Cassandra's for the week. A whole week alone at home would be awful for you, especially since Milly is going to be staying with the neighbours, the McDonalds. Instead, you and I will stay here with Cassandra and keep your candles lit, and give you all the apples and lemonade you could ever need. Look, she's even knitted you a scarf to keep you comfortable!" Katherine held up a giant green scarf, which Gargoth eyed suspiciously. He held out a claw, however, and took the scarf without saying anything. He let it fall beside his cushion.

"It's more of a blanket, wouldn't you say, Katherine?" he said wryly.

"Gargoth says thanks, Cassandra." Katherine hated lying. But she really wanted him to stay for the week, then she and her parents wouldn't have to worry about him getting lonely, or into trouble, or worse, noticed by the neighbours.

Finally Gargoth sighed and said, "Very well, Katherine. I'll stay here for the week with you. I will continue to light the candles at night. Of course, I won't be able to talk much to our kind friend here, since she doesn't understand a word I say. Won't she find me rather dull company?"

Katherine looked over at Cassandra, who was in turn studying the little gargoyle with a look of rapture on her face, and smiled.

"No, I don't think for a second she'll find your company dull. Just stay up here on the roof, and everything will be fine. I'll be at soccer camp all day, but I'll be back every night after dinner, except for the nights I have practice. Or games. Well, I guess I'll be away most of the time, but here at bedtime… It'll be fine."

"Yes, very well. You can tell her she'll have her own gargoyle for the week. Now, let's get back to the story. Where were we?"

Katherine thought for a moment. "You and Philip were crossing the English Channel to France."

"Yes. We did cross the ocean. I won't tell you more about that awful experience except to say it was a calm day, which was just as well, since that tiny boat creaked and shook and jolted and bucked just as though the seas were fierce. And some abominable woman had a basketful of noisy geese. Thankfully, we arrived safely in the French town of Calais."

Gargoth paused and took a long drink of lemonade.

"The next part of our journey was very difficult. Philip walked, with me in the sack on his back, for many weeks through the fields and valleys of France. He had enough money from the sale of the horse and cart to buy food, since the apples were long gone. We slept in farmhouses and village inns, or under the open skies.

"Eventually, we came to the tiny village we sought and began new lives, apart.

"But soon it wasn't so important to me to see Philip, for after a very short time, my life changed forever."

Gargoth's Story, 1665
Le Village Ensemble

Philip was weary and footsore, but he didn't put down his sack. He carried it over his shoulder, despite his exhaustion. He had been walking all night, and it seemed like days since he had left his bed at the last small village inn. He was very tired of small villages and their crowded inns, especially since he didn't understand anything anyone said to him. For the most part, they didn't understand him, either.

Just as he crested a long, steep hill, he came upon a wooden signpost which read:

Ensemble, 2

The village of Ensemble! He and Gargoth had found it, the place they had sought for weeks. He'd lost track of how long he and his little hidden friend had been on the road, searching for this place. The weather was turning colder, much colder, and they had left his village in England when the trees were just starting to change into their autumn colours.

So it must have been five or six weeks. He had lost count. As he trudged slowly along the dark road, Philip heard Gargoth snoring gently in the sack and

56

felt happy to have his friend with him. It would have been a much lonelier journey without him. Gargoth was a great storyteller and helped Philip pass the long hours of walking by making up fantastic tales about the world and the animals living in it beyond the seas. Some nights, sleeping together in the dark, he was glad to know his strange friend was nearby.

The lane Philip was walking along took a sharp turn to the right and suddenly opened up to a tiny valley, with small houses and farms dotted here and there.

The village!

The sun was just about to break above the hills. He wanted to rush into the valley and embrace the first person he saw, but he restrained himself. He was almost fourteen years old, after all. He would need to act like a man, since he most certainly would be treated like one and be expected to work like one by his uncle.

He stood for a moment taking in the sight before him. The first rays of the sun struck over the hill and shone on Philip's face. He shook the apple sack on his shoulder gently.

"Gargoth. Gargoth! Wake up!" After a few more shakes, Philip heard the familiar snap and growl of the little gargoyle waking up.

"What? Is it another cow in the lane?" Gargoth said nastily.

"No, it's not a cow. We're here. We've found Ensemble." Philip opened the sack, and Gargoth popped his face out, looking down into the village below them.

"It is pretty, Philip," Gargoth said sleepily. The rising sun was washing the small valley with light, and they could hear the distant sound of cows and sheep, and people rising to tend to them.

"Yes, it is. Very pretty."

Philip closed the sack again (although Gargoth wasn't happy about it) and walked down the hill. As luck would have it, the village church was at the foot of the hill before them. He opened the gate, which squeaked almost as loudly as the church gate back in England, and carried his sack to the back of the churchyard.

"Look, Gargoth! Apples!" Philip called. Sure enough, an apple orchard stood proudly beside the church. Each tree still had a few late fall apples hanging on the boughs.

"And a river!" he exclaimed again. A small, dark river gamboled along beside the orchard. "You'll have food and water all winter long," Philip said helpfully.

Gargoth clambered out of the sack and stood looking at his friend. They had travelled so far together and had comforted each other so often in the haystacks and muddy lanes of England. They had crossed the English Channel together (an adventure Gargoth would be happy never to repeat) and had walked for weeks to find this tiny, unlikely place.

Philip looked down into Gargoth's face and was surprised to see tears there. He frowned and thought for a moment. Then he put his hand gently on Gargoth's head.

"It's all right, Gargoth," he said quietly. "I'll be back. My family lives somewhere in this valley. I'll find them, then be back to visit you, I promise."

"Yes, Philip. We will see each other soon, no doubt."

Gargoth offered Philip his claw, but Philip laughed

and picked up the little gargoyle, hugging him tight.

"I don't care if you don't like it, Gargoth. I'm giving you a hug, and you can squirm all you want." Philip released the little gargoyle, who strangely didn't fight to get away.

"Goodbye, Gargoth, see you soon! Be safe—stay hidden!" And with that Philip turned away, closed the church gate behind him, and walked down the hill into the valley, ready to start his new life.

"Goodbye, Philip," Gargoth said quietly, then turned to face the church. "I am used to being alone," he whispered.

Gargoth's Story, 1665
The Batless Belfry

It snowed that first night in Ensemble.

After Philip left him in the churchyard that morning, Gargoth climbed the thick ivy clinging to the walls of the church and clambered up to the church tower. He sat there all that first day, looking out over the small valley, growing familiar with the sounds and smells of the village below him. The church was quite far from the village, so there was no chance of anyone catching Gargoth by surprise.

No one did come that first day, though. He quickly understood that the church was empty, perhaps only used on days of worship. That was good news, but small comfort. Now that he was used to having a friend, he understood what it was to miss someone.

That first night Gargoth hid in the church belfry, away from the gently falling snow. Except for the large, glistening bronze church bell, there was nothing else there, not even bats. He was completely alone.

Which was why he was so surprised the next morning, when he woke to find a single beautiful apple waiting at his feet on the floor of the belfry. He was tired, that much was true. But he was quite sure that he had not picked himself an apple for breakfast the day before. In fact, he hadn't left the safety of the church tower and belfry at all since he'd arrived.

It was strange.

During the day, he went into the apple orchard and picked himself a few wizened apples, but they were of poor quality, nothing like the delicious fruit he'd had for breakfast.

Later he sat in the belfry, drumming his claw gently on the giant bronze bell. He looked out over the valley and fell asleep wondering where Philip was sleeping and what his family was doing.

The next morning he woke to find another beautiful apple waiting at his feet, this time accompanied by a jug of sweet water.

Gargoth reached out to the water and took a long drink. It was much better than the brackish water in the river, which he had tasted. And the apple once again was delicious and sweet and nothing like the shrivelled apples on the trees in the orchard.

All that third day, he searched every inch of the church, hoping to find whoever was leaving gifts for him. But he found nothing, other than a heap of apple cores in the bush beside the orchard and a cemetery filled with forgotten beehives and ancient gravestones dusted with snow. That night in the belfry, he fell asleep wishing he could find some tobacco, since his pouch had been empty for weeks. That at least would be some comfort.

The next morning, he woke to find two beautiful

apples, beside another full water jug. And a pouch full of fine tobacco.

Gargoth couldn't believe his eyes. He sat up and slowly drew the tobacco toward him. It was too strange. He had thought about tobacco, and there it was the next day waiting for him.

Someone knew him very well. He wondered if Philip was playing tricks on him, but he would certainly hear the boy entering the churchyard (even if the gate wasn't creaky) and climbing to the belfry. Humans were very loud, even when they were trying to be silent.

Gargoth, though puzzled, didn't waste any time lighting a pipe and eating his apples. He might as well be comfortable, if confused.

But he was making a plan. After finishing his pipe, he curled himself up with his wings tightly drawn around him. He would sleep all day and lie awake that night, waiting for his silent guest.

That night, after a full day of sleep, Gargoth walked around the church tower and tried to look as though he were getting ready to rest when it grew dark. He lay down in his regular place beside the belfry wall and drew his wings tightly around him. Occasionally, he let out a gentle snore, which he hoped sounded realistic.

Nothing happened. For hours, Gargoth pretended to sleep but heard and saw nothing.

Then there was something. It must have been a few hours before sunrise, because it was very dark and cold, and he was sore and cramped from pretending to be asleep all night.

Suddenly his sharp ears caught a faint, odd sound

of wings. A bird, perhaps? But this was not a gentle beating of wings. It was instead a heavy, laboured beating of wings. Odd wings. Clumsy wings.

Leathery wings.

In the darkness, Gargoth could feel something moving very, very slowly toward him on the floor. He stayed perfectly still, straining to hear.

When the intruder was close to him, and he could hear first one apple, then two, then three, being carefully placed on the floor near him, he couldn't wait another second.

He spoke quietly. "You had better tell me who you are, friend or foe. And be quick!" With that, he jumped to his feet and grabbed the intruder by the throat.

A small voice said, "Hamithin sorken behem. Nosta amica. Memamont fella Ambergine."

But Gargoth heard the sweet voice say, "Stay, do not fear. I am a friend. My name is Ambergine."

Gargoth's Story, 1665
The Bell Rings

Gargoth was so startled to hear his own language, he loosened his grip on the throat of the intruder.

Many things happened next.

Ambergine was frightened and struggled to fly to the top of the belfry. Gargoth, in his surprise, tripped over the water jug and spilled it over the hard, dark floor. Then he slipped in the water and fell on the apples Ambergine had just laid out for him. The loud noise of the tipped water jug and the grunt from Gargoth falling hard upon the apples startled Ambergine and caused her wings to falter (she wasn't a great flier at the best of times). She drooped low in the air above Gargoth's head, just as he was clawing the air trying to regain his feet. In his desperation, he grasped her leg and drew her even further from the air. She shrieked and grabbed the first thing she found, which unfortunately was the bell rope for the large bronze church bell beside them.

GONG! GONG! GONG! The bell began to sound, ringing out loudly over the entire valley. This brought both gargoyles to their senses. Ambergine dropped to the ground beside Gargoth, who had finally found his feet on the slippery floor. They both stood frozen to the spot, their chests heaving.

It was Gargoth who spoke first, a few moments later. "What have you done? What will happen now?" he whispered.

"I…I do not know," Ambergine answered. "I have never pulled the bell rope before…" The gargoyles suddenly heard the distant noise of people yelling. They looked at each other for the first time. Gargoth saw a sweet, wide face and deep, deep dark eyes. The gargoyle before him was slightly smaller than he, but very like him in many ways. She too had leathery wings, claws and a small pouch at her side. He was about to speak again when a loud shout from the churchyard gate made them both jump.

Ambergine crept to the edge of the belfry wall and peeked over into the darkness.

"The villagers are here!" she cried. "They will find us!"

Gargoth looked about him and quickly decided what to do. "Out here," he said, drawing Ambergine along with him. They climbed over the belfry wall and down the ivy-covered stones to the back of the church. Just as the villagers opened the church gate, the two little gargoyles scurried into the old abandoned apple orchard, losing themselves in the dark trees.

And just in time. In moments the church was crawling with villagers. Men and boys of all ages were searching the church and belfry for intruders.

Gargoth and Ambergine huddled together in the apple orchard, listening to the villagers comb the church and churchyard just a few breadths from their hiding spot. Soon they heard footsteps approaching.

"Stay silent, no matter what happens," Gargoth whispered.

A heavy footstep, then a lighter one, came closer and closer. They heard a voice say, "I will search the apple orchard, uncle," and the light footsteps approached. They could make out a figure entering the trees just feet from them, and a voice whispered: "Gargoth? Gargoth are you here?"

It was Philip! Gargoth jumped from his hiding spot. In a few short strides, Philip found him. He bent down and whispered, "I'm so glad you're safe! What were you doing ringing the church bell at four o'clock in the morning?"

"It was an accident, obviously," Gargoth started, but was cut short by someone calling Philip's name.

"I'm here, uncle, in the apple orchard," Philip shouted into the darkness. "I'm still looking!"

Philip turned back to Gargoth. "Are you all right?" he whispered. Just at that moment, Ambergine came out from her hiding spot behind a tree. Philip gasped, then smiled. "Who are you?" he asked.

"I am Ambergine. I have lived here always," the little gargoyle answered shyly.

Philip stood up and looked over his shoulder to the church. He could see in the first glow of dawn that the villagers were congregating near the churchyard gate. His uncle was calling him again.

"I have to go. It's nice to meet you, Ambergine," he whispered. "Will you do me a favour and please take care of my friend, Gargoth?"

"Yes, I will. I will, always," she said sombrely, nodding her head and locking her dark eyes on his.

They heard voices approaching. "Be safe, both of you. I'll see you one day soon," Philip whispered, then he turned and strode from the orchard. Gargoth and Ambergine heard him say loudly to a group of nearby men, "There isn't anyone in the orchard, I looked everywhere."

Soon the gargoyles heard the church gate click shut for the last time, and the sound of the villagers' voices dying away as they left the church behind for the comfort of their beds.

When they were alone, Gargoth turned to Ambergine. "It's nice to meet you, Ambergine," he said. They both burst into laughter.

And if you've ever heard two gargoyles burst into laughter, you know it sounds just like two long-lost friends who have found each other at last.

Chapter Thirteen
Lentils Forever

Katherine's plan worked out perfectly. Her parents were on their way to Saskatoon, and she and Gargoth were staying with Cassandra at Candles By Daye for the week. Soccer camp started the next morning.

On their first day together, Katherine settled in the spare bedroom at the back of the store and shared her first dinner with Cassandra. At dinnertime Katherine was surprised (and a little worried) to discover that Cassandra was a vegetarian. Katherine found it odd that in all their time together, this fact had never come up, but it did explain why Cassandra never ate much when she visited their house for barbecues. Katherine suddenly felt horrified at all the times she or her mother or father had held a huge plate of steak in front of Cassandra, offering her something off the grill. *Good thing she's so sweet,* she thought.

Cassandra's meal consisted of mashed chick peas and lentils, which Katherine picked at gingerly. She moaned to herself that she was going to eat *a lot* of lentils during the week (and enviously looked over at Gargoth, who was gorging himself on apples, the only thing she had ever seen him eat). But since she had tortured Cassandra with steaks, she thought it was only fair that Cassandra get to torture her with lentils.

Katherine was sure that her tall friend was really happy to have them there and wanted everything to be perfect for them both.

That was difficult, because it was hard to make anything perfect for Gargoth. If you cared too much, you were liable to be hurt by his indifference. Katherine didn't want to spend all week making excuses for Gargoth's rudeness, but she'd do it if she had to. She was so grateful to Cassandra for keeping her in Toronto, and to her parents for letting her go to soccer camp (and not to a wedding of people she'd never met) that she'd do whatever it took. She would eat lentil stew. She would eat lentil soup. She would eat lentil cake and drink lentil tea, if there was such a thing. And be happy she was in Toronto.

On their first night as Cassandra's guests, they relaxed on the rooftop amid blazing pumpkin candles. It was a soft, beautiful evening. Gargoth wiggled on his cushion, looking at the stars. Some of the candles had burned down to nearly nothing. Cassandra carried another box of pumpkin candles to the rooftop so Gargoth could replace any that had burned too low.

Cassandra was knitting and Katherine was thinking about what her soccer camp might be like the next day, when Gargoth spoke. "I think I should finish my story, Katherine. It is almost at an end. Where was I?"

Katherine thought for a while, then asked Cassandra. "What was the last thing I told you?"

Cassandra said immediately, "Gargoth and Philip made it to Ensemble, and Gargoth found Ambergine in the church. Well, I think you actually said that she found him."

"Yes, that was it. You and Philip found the village, and you found Ambergine. Well, she found you." Katherine and Cassandra waited as Gargoth shifted again. Katherine sensed that he was reluctant to speak. After a long pause, he cleared his throat.

"Yes, Ambergine found me. Right from the moment we met in the church belfry, we were inseparable. We were friends, brother and sister, sun and moon, black and white. She was as sweet as I was nasty. She was as kind as I was mean. She never doubted that we would be together always. Over the years, I began to forget what it was to be lonely.

"Very soon we discovered that we both carried the mark of the stonemason Tallus, and that made us closer than friends. We were family. Philip came to visit us now and then, and as he grew to be a man, then the head of a family, then an old country gentleman, he never failed to visit us on special occasions, or the first days of spring. When he was a very old man, he brought a young boy to meet us, his grandson Marcus.

"One day I saw a group of people dressed in black, gathered around a gravestone in the churchyard. Young Marcus was among them and found me secretly to tell me that his Grandfather Philip had died. I perched for many days and nights on Philip's grave, only to discover a new pain which Ambergine called 'sorrow'. I knew that no amount of faithful waiting would return my friend to me, though at times I see his happy face before me still…" Gargoth's voice grew quiet. He shifted on his cushion, silent for a few moments, deep in thought.

"But we were not alone, since Marcus came now and then to visit us, bringing news of the world. In turn, Marcus grew to old age and chose a grandson to befriend us. For generations it went on. Ambergine and I lived in Ensemble for more than a hundred years, together and happy, safely hidden in the church belfry.

"And so we would still be today, if not for Ambergine's desire to see the world."

Clearly he didn't want to go on, but Katherine asked him gently, "What happened then?"

With sadness in his voice, Gargoth said, "We left Ensemble. Philip's great-grandson was a world traveller, and he told Ambergine wonderful stories of Europe and the composer Mozart. She wanted so badly to hear his music and to see the city of Paris that I finally agreed to be taken to that great place. We stowed away together in Philip's great-grandson's horse and cart one spring day, leaving our churchyard home. It was 1778, and Ambergine and I would never see Ensemble again."

Gargoth's voice was full of longing and sadness, and his head was turned away from his listeners. Even Cassandra, who could not understand a word, caught the change in his tone and dropped her knitting into her lap to look at him.

"Instead we lived at the great cathedral of Notre Dame in Paris."

"Oh, yes! I've heard of it! That's where all the famous gargoyles are!" Katherine jumped in.

Gargoth shot her a withering look. "Famous? Maybe. But dead. Not a single living gargoyle, just lifeless creatures of stone. I know because we lived among them for decades. We heard Mozart play his Paris Symphony, which was all the rage the summer of 1778. We heard the beautiful music lifting gently over the city to our home high atop the cathedral.

"We watched Paris go through a bloody revolution and a terrible war. We survived more plague and famine and disease.

"And then one night, disaster came to Notre Dame." These last words Gargoth spat out bitterly.

"What happened?" Katherine asked, shocked.

"Thieves, Katherine. And my own failure…"

Here Gargoth fell silent and would not speak again. It was the end of his story, and despite her best efforts, Katherine could not get him to say another word. She told Cassandra everything he had said, and although she didn't want to leave, she finally had no choice. She would have an entire day of soccer the next day, and she needed to get to sleep. She stood, hugged Cassandra, then said softly, "Goodnight, Gargoth. See you in the morning."

But she may as well have saved her breath. Gargoth lay silent on his cushion, and except for the heaving of his little shoulders as he wept, he was still as stone. If he had been able to finish his story, this is what he would have said…

Gargoth's Story, 1860
Thieves Take All

It was very early morning. The great bell had just stopped ringing the hour.

Gargoth rapped his claws against the cold stone wall before him. He was looking into the streets and alleys far below him, down to the foot of the great Notre Dame cathedral. The waking city of Paris lay at his feet. He was surrounded by an army of stone statues, most of them strange and frightening animals, lions and huge birds of prey. Here and there were also grotesque and bizarre gargoyles.

They were a bit like him, but none had his fine features, or his leathery skin, or his pouch. Most of them were simply rainspouts, there to direct water into the street far below. Gargoth had watched many times as unsuspecting people in the streets were soaked by the gargoyles spouting rainwater far above them.

And none of the statues was alive.

He leaned over the stone wall, intently watching a child in the street far below him. The child was alone and begging for food from passersby. No one stopped to help him, though, even people who looked as if they had plenty of food to spare. The street was very busy with people going here and there, and many were carrying baskets overflowing with bread or apples or cheese. The stores were just beginning to open, and merchants, bakers, farmers and storekeepers were bringing their wares into the streets and to the square before the cathedral.

But no one would help the small beggar boy.

Gargoth watched for a while with a deep frown upon his face. Eventually he turned away and waddled to an alcove in the stone wall, a hidden cave behind the stone statues.

Ambergine was inside. She had just come back from a night-time raid on the local apple orchard and was emptying out her pouch, which was bulging with apples.

Gargoth walked to her side and put out his claw. "Apple," he grunted. She placed an apple in his claw and followed him out into the statues and back to the wall.

Gargoth was sizing up the child on the street far below again.

ZING! The apple flew and landed near the child. It rolled harmlessly to the boy's feet. They both watched as the child fell upon the apple and ran off, taking big bites as he ran.

"He's new," Ambergine sighed.

"Is he? I hadn't noticed. He looks like all the others to me." Gargoth began rapping his claws on the stone wall once again, looking out over the streets and alleys of Paris as the rich and poor lived out their lives below him.

None of them knew there were living gargoyles high above them, keeping watch over them all.

Ambergine went back to the stone cave for her breakfast. She chewed quietly on an apple. She didn't want to tell Gargoth about a troubling incident in the orchard a few nights before. She had quietly been picking apples when she'd heard some men talking nearby. They had very rough voices and sounded like dangerous and unpleasant men.

One man was saying, "I saw it too. Just there—like a great flying bat."

The other said, "Yes, and it wasn't the first time. I heard the farmer say he sees this great bat all the time."

Ambergine froze as she realized the men were talking about her. She stayed very quiet, hidden in an apple tree as they searched the orchard at her feet, but they didn't find her.

As soon as she could, she flew away into the darkness, flying from treetop to treetop until she made it back to the cathedral and safety.

But she couldn't shake a sense of worry. She had been especially careful the night before in the orchard but couldn't help feeling that she was being followed.

It would be difficult to follow her there, though. There were 422 long stone steps between them and the street far below, and humans rarely visited their part of the cathedral, except once in a while when a few men climbed up to a tiny wooden doorway nearby. It was their job to inspect the ancient bricks and walls at the top of the cathedral, to make sure they weren't crumbling into the streets below. It was the only time Gargoth and Ambergine had to worry about being discovered.

They were among hundreds of stone statues and

gargoyles, after all. If someone came upon them, they simply had to stay still and blend in. It was the perfect place for a pair of gargoyles to stay hidden and safe.

The rest of that day went by as usual. The two gargoyles slept then kept the pigeons off the nearby statues (for who wanted to live with pigeons fouling everything?). They sat and listened to the music of the evening chapel fill the air and talked quietly together amid the beautiful voices rising in song. Gargoth smoked his pipe in peaceful silence.

As that warm fall day faded into glowing early evening, the gargoyles were playing Troll-my-Dame (a kind of very old game of marbles) with small rounded stones. Ambergine hardly ever won, since Gargoth was a much better shot than she was.

As it grew dark, she and Gargoth stopped their game and were watching the city below them slowly go to sleep. Suddenly an unusual sound made both gargoyles freeze.

The tiny wooden doorway nearby creaked open. Ambergine looked at Gargoth, who whispered "*Shhh*" at her and started to tiptoe toward the noise.

"No, Gargoth! Come this way," she begged, but he wasn't listening.

He continued toward the noise, curious. "Who would possibly be climbing to the top of the cathedral tonight?" he thought. "The door must have blown open with the breeze."

But Ambergine suddenly grew very worried.

"It's dark enough," Gargoth whispered. "I can hide quickly if I have to." He crept slowly among the statues toward the tiny door. Paris glowed in the background as the sun set in the west.

Ambergine stood beside the opening to their stone cave, listening.

"I saw them up here, tossing apples into the street, just over there," one man said. He had an ugly voice. And she had heard it before!

"Shush, they might've heard you!" another angry voice hissed.

Ambergine was very frightened now. She could just make out Gargoth in the gloom edging towards the voices. She made a quick decision.

She wasn't very big, but she was strong. She planted her squat feet against the stone wall and pushed with all her might. She pushed and pushed. She could feel the ancient brick wall behind her soften and give with her weight. She pushed again, and with a loud, grinding sound, part of the brick wall fell onto the stone floor.

The men stopped and turned toward her. Ambergine saw candle-light flicker over nearby statues as they turned toward the sound. The men began to move toward her, but Gargoth was in the way. They would see him first!

In desperation, Ambergine jumped onto the wall and began to shout, "Hey! Stupid ugly men! Over here!"

Many things happened then. The men shouted and ran toward Ambergine. Gargoth shouted too and jumped from his hiding place, directly into the path of the chasing men. He jumped up onto the wall behind her, and both gargoyles moved as quickly as they could along the wall, almost at a run. But having very short, thick legs, they didn't move fast enough, and in no time the men were upon them.

Gargoth was right behind Ambergine. "RUN! You must! FASTER!" he cried. But it was no use.

Two heavy hands grabbed for Ambergine, who jumped off the wall and flew out of harm's way, hovering high over the city and just out of reach. But Gargoth was surrounded. He looked frantically at Ambergine.

"JUMP, GARGOTH! FLY!" she screamed, but it was too late. As Gargoth hesitated, too afraid to leap off the stone wall and try to fly to safety, a sturdy cloth sack landed over his head.

The thieves had their prize. They laughed to hear the little flying gargoyle sob and cry, and they shook Gargoth's cloth sack cruelly. They took him far away and sold him to traders who stole him over the ocean. He began a new life many, many months later, in New York City, lonely, lost and dejected without Ambergine. He refused to speak, eat or drink for many months, but none of his captors cared enough to notice.

It was 1860, and he would be held prisoner alone a long, long time. Over the dreary years, Gargoth would change hands many times and had many different owners. His first owner was a sea captain who lost Gargoth in a card game. His second was a circus ringmaster who made him dance for the circus performers after dark. The next was a kindly travelling vendor, and a friend. The fourth, and last, was a horrible, spoiled, heartbroken little boy who lived in a dark mansion above New York City and who grew into a horrible, lonely, twisted old man. He was Gargoth's greatest enemy.

He calls himself The Collector, and if you've been paying close attention (which I'm sure you have), although you've just learned his name, you've already met him in this story three times. He's been watching and waiting, hiding and sneaking, with one thing on his mind: he wants Gargoth back, and he doesn't care what he has to do, or who he has to hurt, to get him. Which is how he got Gargoth in the first place…

Gargoth's Story, 1939
What Happened at
The World's Fair

The fairgrounds were alive with people from all over the world. They had come to see the greatest fair the world had ever known: The World's Fair, New York City, 1939. It was the fair which promised to show everyone "The World of Tomorrow".

A small boy held his father's hand tightly as they worked their way through the throng of people. The boy wished he were back in his dark home, far above the city, and far from the press of people all around him. It was too bright and noisy for his liking. He adjusted his thick glasses (he had very poor vision) and held tighter to his father.

But they *had* seen some interesting things in the great buildings and in the huge sphere, called the Perisphere. There had been an exciting new invention called "television", where they'd seen President Roosevelt say words and move around on a little grey screen. They had also seen Elecktro, a seven foot tall walking, talking robot, and a futuristic miniature replica of New York City.

But what the boy liked most were the statues, since

they were quiet and still. They didn't mock his rich clothes or laugh at his thick glasses like the children in school. He already had a small collection of statues at home: they were his only friends and didn't talk back.

There were statues all over the fairgrounds, huge statues of gods and kings and mythical creatures, and the boy wanted one.

He tugged at his father's sleeve. "Papa, I want a statue." His father looked down at him, through his own thick glasses, and smiled.

"Another statue? What do you want this time?"

"I want a mifical creature."

"You mean 'mythical', and I haven't seen a pavilion selling statues. How about a replica of the Perisphere?" His father stopped and handed him a small white sphere from a table.

They were standing in front of a vendor's stall. Like every other stall, or pavilion, or tent selling things, this vendor was selling small statues of the Perisphere and Trylon and Helicline—all replicas of exhibits at the Fair. The owner of the stall looked up and grinned.

"Yes, how about a Perisphere for the young man?" he said, winking at the boy. The boy scowled and looked away. He was used to getting whatever he wanted. His father was rich enough to buy him anything he ever asked for. He wasn't about to settle for a small, insignificant trinket, sold to him by a man who might have been somebody's servant.

"No," he pouted. He pointed across the road to a large statue of a winged horse, standing high above the crowds. "I want that one."

The boy's father and the vendor both laughed. The boy's pout grew darker.

"You can't have that one. That's a gift from the people of France, and it's made of marble. Even I couldn't buy you that statue. Pick something smaller."

The boy stomped his foot. "NO! I WANT THAT ONE!" he screamed. He did not like being laughed at, and he did not like not getting his own way.

His father knelt down, his expensive coat mixing with the mud of the fairgrounds and with a worried look tried to calm the boy. "Son, I can't buy you that one…surely you can understand that?"

"NO! I DON'T! I WANT IT!" the boy screamed even louder, turning purple in the face. He was making so much noise that a crowd was beginning to gather, staring and laughing at the small boy having a tantrum.

The father stood up abruptly and shouted at the vendor. "What else do you have that my son might like?"

The shocked vendor shook his head and shrugged. "Nothing. I only sell these Perispheres. Sorry, mister." But there was something in the man's look that made the rich man draw closer. He drew his face up to the vendor's, all the while holding his squalling son's sweaty palm.

"What's that, then?" he asked angrily, pointing his free hand at a partly covered cage at the back of the vendor's stall. The vendor moved quickly to cover the cage completely, but it was too late: the rich man had seen it and sensed it was something of worth.

"What do you have in that cage there?" he demanded.

"Nothing. Really, it's nothing you'd be interested in, believe me," the vendor answered, sounding desperate.

"You're going to show me what's in that cage. Do you have any idea who I am? I'm one of the richest men in New York City, I could buy you and your whole family. Show me the cage…"

The vendor sighed and slowly pulled the cloth off the cage, closing the cage door with a click and turning a large, shiny key inside the lock. He held the cage up to the man and the boy.

"See, it's nothing. Just a gargoyle statue, and a small one at that. Nothing that a rich man like you would be interested in."

The man looked with disgust at the statue in the cage and snorted his contempt. But the boy dropped his father's hand and drew closer. He stuck his finger in the cage and poked at the statue.

"Why is it in this cage?" the boy demanded after a few moments.

"I do a lot of travelling. It's fragile, I don't want it to break. It's safest in there," the vendor answered quickly.

"You're lying. It's special…" The boy picked up the cage and shook it. The statue rattled around inside.

The vendor drew in his breath but said nothing.

As the boy continued to shake and rattle the cage and poke at the statue inside, the rich man pulled the vendor to one side and whispered, "Look, my son is rude, I know, but he has just lost his mother. He has a fondness for statues, he is collecting them, it is the only thing that makes him happy. What are the cage and the gargoyle statue worth? I will pay you two times what you ask…" The rich man drew out his wallet and looked beseechingly at the vendor.

"He's…it's not really for sale," the vendor stammered. "It's just a worthless keepsake, of sentimental value only to me…it's worthless to anyone else, really…"

Suddenly a scream filled the air. "IT BIT ME!"

The father ran to his son's side. The boy was sucking his finger, tears shining on his face, clasping the cage to his chest.

"What do you mean, it bit you? It's a lump of clay…" The father looked up at the vendor, suddenly furious at the man.

"What's going on here?" he demanded of the salesman. "I'll sue you! I'll ruin you! What kind of a thing is this? It hurt my son! It should be destroyed!"

But he was very surprised to see the man collapse into a puddle of tears and hear his son's now-quiet voice say, "It's okay, Papa. I want it. Make the man give it to me. I want to take it home…"

"Fine then," the rich man said, swooping down on his son and swirling away from the vendor and his tiny stall. He threw some bills into the man's face and shouted over his shoulder. "We're taking the cage and the statue, and you're not going to stop us. You're lucky I don't have you arrested…"

And with that, the boy and his father melted back into the crowd, the vendor watching them go.

"Goodbye, Gargoth," he whispered sadly, tears in his eyes.

The boy had what he wanted and clutched the cage, happy now, oblivious to the vendor's sadness or the little gargoyle weeping inside.

It will be years before the boy lets Gargoth out of

the cage, even for a moment. And it will be longer still, seventy years or more, before Gargoth sees a friendly face again.

Chapter Fourteen
Ball-on-a-foot

It was a clear night in Toronto. Cassandra was watching Katherine play soccer. Katherine's team was playing against a team of tall girls, and her team was losing 3-0. It wasn't a great game.

At Cassandra's feet was a sturdy yellow canvas backpack. If you looked closely, you might notice two dark holes cut into the cloth, but you probably wouldn't look that closely. It was just an old backpack, after all. Certainly, no one had ever noticed the holes or commented on them. Occasionally they might think they heard an odd sound coming from it, something like a whispery breeze or a sneeze or cough, but then they dismissed it. It was awfully loud sitting on the sidelines of a soccer game, and it was hard to tell where noises came from, exactly.

Of course it was Gargoth inside, calling out encouragement (or more often saying something rude to the opposite team). Thankfully no one understood him, and when Gargoth became too loud or outrageous, Cassandra would gently pat the backpack, reminding him to be quiet.

It worked perfectly. No one knew Gargoth was there.

Everyone was cheerful (despite the losing score), and people were chatting and commenting on the game, but if you looked closely (if you were the type to look closely enough to notice holes cut into a backpack, for instance), you might notice an old man sitting off by himself all alone, watching the game. He wore thick glasses, a white straw hat and a big baggy brown jacket which didn't fit with the hot weather. Most of the time he stared straight ahead, but sometimes he would suddenly stare up into the night sky, as though he was expecting rain, which was odd, since it was a perfectly clear evening.

And once in a while he turned to look over at Cassandra Daye. Or really, at the yellow canvas backpack at her feet.

If you looked even more closely, say with a telescope or binoculars (not completely unheard of at a soccer game), you might notice a tiny winged creature circling high, high above the soccer field, then flying slowly off into the night.

Chapter Fifteen
Ambergine:
In Toronto with the Dwarves

Ambergine flew, clumsily perhaps, but she flew…

She was circling slowly, high above the city, searching for anywhere a gargoyle would want to hide. She had visited the Golden Nautilus store the night before but found nothing. No gargoyles at all. Plenty of odd statues and frightening masks and candles and incense. But no gargoyles.

Her hiding place for the past few days had been a large round park with a giant statue of a poet in it. She curled up beside the poet's head each day, perfectly hidden.

This night, she was flying over a neighbourhood west of the university with many small backyards. She had just flown over a large field full of girl children running after a strange black and white ball. She had seen this odd human game played many times in her life, but it didn't really interest her, so she left.

She flew lower, just skimming the tops of the trees. As she flew, she heard a quiet trickling coming from one backyard. Water. She decided to investigate and flew lower, hovering just above the yard. The house was dark, so the people were out. She settled on the backyard fence.

What a backyard! It was full of glorious flowers and statues. The trickling was coming from a unicorn fountain; water was pouring from its long, curly horn into a small pool at the unicorn's feet. She hopped off the fence and waddled toward the unicorn. She could use a drink.

She opened the little pouch at her side and pulled out a small jug, which she filled with water. She drank long, then wiped her mouth with her claw and looked around.

There were statues everywhere. Three dwarf statues (on closer inspection, she found one had a badly broken nose recently fixed), a cherub with little wings, and a beautiful apple tree strangely bearing fruit in the middle of the summer. She flew heavily to a bough in the tree and decided to help herself. She picked a few apples and breathed in their scent, which was heavenly. She placed them in the pouch at her side for later.

As she picked another apple and took an enormous bite, she noticed something odd. There was an empty stone pedestal beside the back fence. There was also a bench beside it, just as though friends sat and talked there all the time.

Ambergine flew over for a closer look and stopped dead.

A calico cat was eyeing her from the bushes near the empty pedestal. Ambergine didn't particularly like cats, nor, in her experience, did cats particularly like her. Most of the time they ran away from her.

Occasionally, a very brave cat might stand its ground and spit at her.

But this cat did neither of these things. Instead, the cat walked over to Ambergine and rubbed itself against her legs.

"Well, you *are* an odd creature," said Ambergine surprised, reaching down and stroking the cat's head with her claw. "Aren't you supposed to be afraid of me?"

But this cat was not afraid. In fact, when Ambergine hopped up onto the pedestal, the cat jumped up and sat in her lap. Ambergine was oddly comforted by the little cat purring in her lap. She stroked the cat's fur for a while, quite comfortable.

But suddenly the cat jumped down. The neighbour's back door opened, and a man's voice called, "Milly! Milly kitty! Time to come in! C'mere, kitty!"

The little cat looked back up at Ambergine, whisked its tail, then trotted off to be let into the neighbour's house.

"How strange," Ambergine thought. But that wasn't all that seemed strange to her. It was beginning to dawn on her that this yard was special. There was something familiar and comforting about it.

This yard had water, apples, an empty pedestal and a cat which wasn't afraid of her.

It would make a perfect place for a gargoyle to live.

Just then a loud noise in the alley startled her. A man's voice cursed in the dark.

Ambergine streaked to the top of the apple tree. A man with a white straw hat, a big baggy jacket and thick glasses stood by the back fence, peering into the yard. He looked up at her in the tree.

Ambergine shrieked and took off into the night. She flew as far and as fast as she could. She didn't stop flying for hours, and when she finally collapsed from exhaustion on the roof of a tiny library, she had no idea where she was.

Life is unfair sometimes. If she had flown just a few rooftops further, she would have come across one hundred and forty-eight orange-scented pumpkin candles burning low, late into the night.

Chapter Sixteen
Gargoth and Cassandra

The week with Cassandra went very slowly for Gargoth. He lay about on the rooftop of the store, being as polite as he could, drinking the lemonade and eating the apples which his kind host left out for him night after night. The only time he had spent with Katherine was the night before when they had gone to her soccer game.

Each evening, Cassandra and Gargoth would light the beacon together, then they would sit silently while Cassandra worked on her knitting and Gargoth smoked his pipe and stared into the sky. Eventually Gargoth would get up and blow out the candles, and Cassandra would say goodnight then descend the stairs to her apartment at the back of the store.

But it was odd without Katherine there. She was away all day, only to come home too late and tired to do anything but eat and go straight to bed. He had no way to communicate with Cassandra, and he found her great height and clumsiness oddly upsetting. One night, he heard a great crash below him and hurried down the steep stairs to see what had happened. He was in such a hurry that he tumbled down the last few stairs and landed heavily on his back. He grunted and struggled to right himself, only to find Cassandra fussing over him, completely unhurt herself. She had dropped something and had come to no harm. Gargoth was the one who was hurt.

So he remained steadfastly on the roof after that, no matter what noises came from down below. Cassandra had put a small tent on the roof for him to sleep in. She called it a "pup tent", which made him feel uncomfortably like a dog, but he didn't complain. It was dry and cozy enough with his cushion in there to sleep on.

In the daytime, people would come and go in the store below, announcing themselves with a little tinkle of the doorbell as they entered. Cassandra would see to them, sell them a scented candle or a crystal ball or a book about something called "yoga", then a little while later they would let themselves out the door, which would tinkle again. Gargoth got used to the comings and goings down below him and ignored most of what happened there.

Near the end of their week together, however, Gargoth was lying on his cushion, not paying much attention to the shop below, when he heard the sound of angry voices. He sat up and listened carefully.

A man's voice was raised loudly. "I know that you have something of mine. You ought to give it back. You are stealing from me! It's my property!"

Cassandra's voice shot back, "I have no idea what you are talking about. We don't have any here, can't you see? Now you should really leave, or I'll phone the police!" Gargoth couldn't see her, but he felt sure that

Cassandra was standing at her full height, over six feet, and looking very fierce.

For a moment Gargoth was filled with gratitude for Cassandra. He had no idea what was going on, but he was very happy that she was courageous and strong. He heard the bell over the door tinkle furiously, and a second later the door slammed hard. The man had left. He heard Cassandra walk across the store and lock the door.

Gargoth descended a few steps and peered over the edge of the stairway to the shop below. Cassandra was standing beneath him, clutching the store counter with one hand, pushing her curly red hair back from her face with the other. She looked very flustered.

"Cassandra?" Gargoth said.

Cassandra looked up at the sound of his whispery voice. "Oh, Gargoth. Did you hear that?" She waved her hand toward the door.

He nodded.

"Oh." She thought for a minute. "Gargoth, you can understand me, correct?"

He nodded again, more slowly this time.

"Okay. Can you nod or shake your head for me, yes or no?"

Another nod.

"Is someone looking for you?"

A shrug.

"Okay, then, let me be more exact. Is it *possible* that someone is looking for you?"

Gargoth looked at his scaly feet for a moment and shrugged again. But he also slowly nodded.

"Would it be an old man?"

A faint nod.

"Does he wear a white straw hat, a big baggy brown jacket and thick glasses?" Cassandra said this with a chill in her voice, but she was silenced by Gargoth's response.

The little gargoyle started making a terrible noise, which could not be mistaken as anything but a heart-broken howl. Cassandra ran up the stairs and stood over him, unsure what to do.

Gargoth was shrieking and sobbing with terror, his entire body curled in fear. Cassandra sat on the stair beside him with a very worried look on her face. Gargoth turned and suddenly buried his little face in her shoulder, scalding her with hot gargoyle tears. She held him tightly while he wept.

It didn't matter whether they understood each other or not; anyone watching would have seen one friend deeply upset, and the other friend doing her best to comfort him.

Chapter Seventeen
Ambergine:
Goldfish and Crabapples

Ambergine rested for three days.

She had gotten over her fright at seeing the man in the white straw hat in the yard with the calico cat. But she had not recovered from flying across the entire city in one night.

In a bit of luck (the only real luck she had had so far), the library rooftop had a garden, with a small goldfish pond in it, and a row of tiny potted trees. She would have plenty of water to drink. There was an ornamental crabapple tree in a container, so she had apples to eat, too (although they were small and awfully sour). She thought this would be a perfect place to rest from her long flight for a few days.

And she didn't see anyone on the roof except one time when a librarian ate her lunch on the bench beside the goldfish pond. Ambergine stayed still as a statue in the garden, and although she was in plain sight, the librarian never noticed her. All in all, it was a perfect spot to hide out, high above the streets.

But she wasn't idle. While she rested between the goldfish pond and the crabapple tree, she was trying to remember what she knew of the man with the white straw hat.

She was trying to remember everything that Gargoth had told her about his greatest enemy. For that is who he was: the man with the white straw hat was Gargoth's last owner, the one who had kept him prisoner for years and years in New York City.

The worst one of all.

She had to concentrate.

What had Gargoth said about him? He was "invincible", that was the word he had used. And he would never give up trying to find Gargoth. He had said that too. He desperately wanted Gargoth back, for some reason.

She couldn't quite remember why. Oh yes. It was because the man knew that Gargoth was alive.

"Because I am alive, he wants me back. I am a curiosity to him, and he will never stop until he finds me. He thinks I am his property. He is very rich, spoiled, and alone. Except for me."

That's what Gargoth had said.

Ambergine took a bite of crabapple and winced. They really were sour. Sometimes she wished she enjoyed eating something else, like night bugs. She had watched many bats over the years, and there were always plenty of bugs for them to eat. She shuddered. She had tried bugs now and then, but they were *much* too crunchy for her taste. And wriggly.

She sighed and looked out toward the glowing city. Toronto was very pretty, she had to admit, but she could never like the city, unless of course she found what she was looking for.

She shook her head and sighed. She *had* found him in New York, eventually, even though both she and Gargoth had almost been killed for her efforts.

Toronto is smaller and quieter than New York; it won't be that *hard to find him, will it?* she wondered, unconvinced. She was growing tired, very tired, of searching.

Chapter Eighteen
This Store is Closed

As the evening drew near, Ambergine was ready to try again to find the backyard with the calico cat.

She had rested for several days, so she was no longer too tired to fly. The water and the crabapples, such as they were, had given her strength.

Each night she had noticed a warm glow from a few rooftops over. She wasn't sure what it was, but she liked the look of it. It was as though many lamps, or perhaps candles, were flickering gently in the night breeze. There was something familiar about it too, although she wasn't entirely sure what it was. She decided if she had the energy, she might fly over to see what was there.

Either way, she would fly again that night, after she took one final long drink and filled her pouch with crabapples.

Meanwhile, inside Candles by Daye, Cassandra had hung a "CLOSED" sign on the front door and was talking on the phone. She was very excited and talking quickly.

"Yes, yes, I don't know. He just came in here in his baggy coat and white straw hat and started demanding that I give him what 'belonged to him.'" Here Cassandra dropped her voice and looked toward the back corner of the store. Gargoth was slumped beside a large Buddha statue, idly playing with coloured sets of healing crystals.

"I think you'd better come quickly. Can you leave soccer camp now? He seems really…sad. I mean sadder than normal. And I can't find out anything more from him, because I can't understand him, so it's been really frustrating for both of us." Cassandra was whispering now. "And the man said something about Gargoth being his property, or some nonsense. We have to get to the bottom of it, Katherine. I'm really worried…" Cassandra trailed off.

Gargoth stood and waddled over to her. He raised his claw, as though to ask for the telephone. Surprised, Cassandra bent down and handed it to him.

Gargoth looked at it suspiciously, but slowly put it to his ear. When he heard nothing, he looked up at Cassandra.

"You have to speak, Gargoth," she said.

"Katherine?" Gargoth uttered slowly.

"Gargoth?" came Katherine's surprised voice.

Gargoth quickly moved the phone away from his ear, but then slowly moved it back, holding it gingerly in his claw. "Yes, Katherine, it is me. I do not want to use this ridiculous talking machine, but I have no choice. Listen carefully. We were just visited by my greatest enemy. Your kind friend showed him the door, but he will be back." Gargoth was hissing now. "He will try to steal me, Katherine. I must go away, now. I am endangering you, and your tall friend here…"

100

Katherine heard Gargoth sob, and she felt a jolt of anger. Who would dare hurt Gargoth? She would do whatever she could to protect him, and she knew Cassandra and her parents would, too.

She said very calmly into her cell phone, "Don't worry, Gargoth. I'm coming to get you. Cassandra and I will always keep you safe, no matter what." She wanted to add, "My mom and dad will, too," but it seemed pointless, since they were so far away.

But the line was dead. Gargoth had said all he had to say.

Katherine clicked her phone shut and ran over to her coach. "I'm sorry, I've got to go, there's an emergency at home," she said, flinging her soccer equipment into her bag and throwing it over her shoulder.

"Everyone okay?" the coach asked, sounding worried.

"Uh, yes, it's my little…brother…he's…uh… running with scissors!" she said, flustered.

Running with scissors? Is that the best I can do?

"I mean, he's hurt. He's okay, but I've got to go. I'll see you on Monday! Thanks!" And she ran to catch the streetcar, which had just rattled into view.

As she sat, Katherine thought about everything that Cassandra and Gargoth had said. It was urgent. It was terrible. Gargoth was in danger! A man in a white straw hat was a terrible enemy, and he knew where Gargoth was! He was looking for him! He wanted him back!

Katherine wasn't sure what she could tell her parents if they came home and found Gargoth gone forever.

Chapter Nineteen
Two at Once

After Gargoth hung up, he returned to the corner beside the Buddha, quiet and sullen. Cassandra put out some water and apples for him and told him she'd be in the back room, sorting a new shipment of tarot cards and Toronto keychains.

She also told him that Katherine would be there really soon. "You'll be safe if you just stay here, okay? I'm right there," she said, pointing to the room behind the hanging beads. "Just call me if you need me." She disappeared behind the beads with a swish of her long skirt.

Gargoth started pacing back and forth between the door and the Buddha statue. He had a scowl on his face.

When a deliveryman banged on the door ten minutes later, he stood very quietly, still as a statue. Cassandra said through the glass, "Sorry, we're closed," as she pointed at the "CLOSED" sign hanging there.

"Lady, I gotta deliver these necklaces now, or you're not gonna get them any time soon. They go back to the wholesaler if I don't drop them off right now." Cassandra sighed and unlocked the door. She had been waiting for months for the necklaces—they were steel blue with skulls and crossbones on them, and for some reason, every teenager in town wanted one.

Cassandra opened the door. The man trundled in with the heavy boxes, which immediately fell and knocked over a large display of essential oils. For a few minutes, Cassandra and the man ran wildly around the store with rags and mops, cleaning up the mess. It seems she had met someone more clumsy than herself.

When they had cleaned up the broken vials of oil, and the man had left, Cassandra looked around for Gargoth.

But there was no sign of him. He was gone.

She ran to the door, frantic, looking up and down the empty street. In one direction, she saw the delivery man putting a few boxes into the back of his van.

In the other direction, she saw the man in the white straw hat running away as fast as he could! A suspicious bulge was wiggling under his baggy brown jacket. She saw something fall from under his jacket, and she dashed to the spot where it had fallen on the sidewalk.

It was Gargoth's pipe, broken in two.

Cassandra shouted, "STOP! Come back!" She ran along the sidewalk to the corner as fast as her long legs could carry her. A lady coming out of a grocery store had to jump out of the way of the careening giantess. A mother pushing a stroller yelped and dashed out of her way, too.

Cassandra ran to the corner, gasping and trying to catch her breath.

But she was too late. The man with the white straw hat hailed a taxi and jumped into the back seat with the struggling lump under his jacket. The last Cassandra saw of him was the taxi whizzing west along Queen Street.

"NO!" shrieked Cassandra. "Come back!" she yelled.

It was no use. The man in the white straw hat was gone. And so was Gargoth.

Cassandra ran back into her store, about to phone the police. If she had been thinking clearly though, she might have rethought that. What was she going to say?

A thief stole my gargoyle, he's about this high, and oh yes, he's alive.

She didn't have a chance to call the police anyway, since just as she sped back into her store, she heard a loud crash from the rooftop. She dashed upstairs.

By this time, Katherine was getting close to the store. Her streetcar rolled along Queen Street at such a snail's pace that she wanted to scream at the driver to step on it. At one point, it was nearly hit by a taxi speeding past them in the other direction.

When Katherine finally got to her stop, she stumbled onto the sidewalk in her haste. Frantic, she ran to the ancient storefront door and pulled out the key around her neck to open it. But there was no need, because the door was hanging open.

If she hadn't been in such a hurry, she might have noticed that was a little odd. Instead she just roared inside, calling "Cassandra, Cassandra!" at the top of her lungs.

"Up here! Up here Katherine!" shouted the familiar voice from the roof.

Katherine ran up the stairs, two at a time. She skidded onto the roof, saying, 'Where is he? Where's Gar…" but stopped mid-sentence.

A gargoyle was sitting on Gargoth's cushion facing Cassandra, but it wasn't Gargoth.

It was Ambergine. And she was weeping.

CHAPTER TWENTY
WHAT AMBERGINE KNOWS

Katherine screeched to a halt in front of Cassandra and the little gargoyle. Kind Cassandra was holding one of the creature's claws and making soothing sounds. Katherine had a look of amazement on her face as she looked at them both. "What's going on, Cassandra? Where's Gargoth?" she asked.

"It's terrible, Katherine! Gargoth snuck off when I had a deliveryman here, and the…and the…and the man in the white straw hat STOLE HIM!" Cassandra was wailing at this point.

Katherine sat down abruptly, tears welling up in her eyes. She turned toward the little weeping gargoyle.

"And of course you're Ambergine. A few moments too late…" Katherine trailed off. The little gargoyle nodded slowly, too overcome to speak. For several moments the three gathered on the rooftop said nothing. Katherine dug in her soccer bag for tissue and passed some to Cassandra.

Then Katherine spoke again. "Welcome, Ambergine. We've waited for months for you, but we never doubted you would come. I'm Katherine Newberry. I guess you've already met Cassandra. We both know Gargoth well. We're his friends."

Ambergine looked up at her. "He is lucky to have friends such as you…thank you," she said quietly in gargoyle. She placed her head in her claws and didn't speak again. Katherine was intrigued by her raspy voice, a slightly higher, sweeter version of Gargoth's. His voice sounded like the wind rustling in the winter leaves, but she sounded more like a breeze through long grass in summer.

The three sat for a few moments, quiet except for the occasional sniffle. The whole city seemed stilled, almost as though it was holding its breath. It was just too unfair. How could Ambergine find this very rooftop, Gargoth's very cushion, at the exact moment that he was stolen away by his greatest enemy?

Katherine felt a kind of helplessness: where *was* he? But she felt a sudden anger too—how *dare* anyone hurt him! She suddenly knew what she had to do.

She paced across the rooftop and knelt before Ambergine.

"We have to do something quickly. Ambergine, do you know this man in the white straw hat? Can we follow him? Do you have any idea where he might be taking Gargoth?"

Ambergine stood up and started waddling around the rooftop. She was lighter and more graceful than Gargoth and was weaving in and out of the candles. She had a frown on her face and was thinking very hard.

"He must be going back to New York City. Where else would he go? Gargoth said that in all the years he was imprisoned in the dark mansion, the man hardly ever left the property."

"Could you find this dark mansion again, Ambergine?" Katherine asked.

The little gargoyle hesitated then slowly nodded. "I *think* so. It's a big place…but …yes…"

"Are you sure? You seem a little doubtful," Katherine asked.

Slowly Ambergine's eyes filled with tears. "I can find it. I know New York City so well… I could fly over it blindfolded. But…"

"But…what is it?" Katherine asked. Ambergine was clearly very reluctant about something.

"Well, I have always searched alone," she finally whispered.

"You're not alone any more, Ambergine," Katherine said. She gently placed her hand on the little gargoyle's leathery shoulder and kept it there.

Chapter Twenty-One
The Long Night

It didn't take long for the two humans and the gargoyle to prepare a plan.

Katherine, Cassandra and Ambergine were going to New York City to find Gargoth.

Cassandra had an old but very dependable van. She used it to drive to suppliers and warehouses, so it was filled with boxes of leftover candles, knick-knacks, scarves and other odd things (like a giant box of Hawaiian shirts and brightly coloured felt hats).

While Cassandra was loading the van, Katherine phoned her parents and left a message on her mom's cell phone.

"Hi, Mom. Hope you're having fun with your cousin…and her daughter. Is she married yet? I think today is the wedding. Uh, just letting you know that Cassandra and I are fine. I mean everything's fine, but we have to take a little trip. We…um…have to find Gargoth. Who, uh, is missing. But we'll find him! Don't worry. Maybe you'd better phone Cassandra as soon as you get this! Bye!"

She hung up quickly. She knew her mom and

dad would want her and Cassandra to go looking for Gargoth, but she also didn't want them to worry. There really wasn't any easy way to tell them that he was missing. And that she and Cassandra were driving off to New York City in an ancient van to try to find him. With Ambergine.

As Cassandra was getting ready, Katherine stayed on the rooftop with Ambergine. She comforted the little gargoyle by telling her everything about Gargoth's life with them for the past year.

"Well, he was really naughty at first. We got to know him after he destroyed our flower garden and damaged a dwarf statue."

Ambergine used a claw to stop a tear trickling down her face. She said shyly, "Yes, he left a trail of broken statues in his wake. I was always fixing them."

Katherine smiled. "Sounds familiar. But he became really good friends with us eventually. In the end, he fixed the flowers and grew a magical apple tree. He even became great friends with our calico cat, Milly."

At this, Ambergine sat up straight, and her dark eyes grew wide with surprise. "Did you say *Milly*?" she asked.

"Yes, our cat's name is Milly."

Ambergine smiled. *I knew it. I* did *find you*. She was pleased for a moment.

"I like his beacon," she said, smiling faintly and waving her claw over the expanse of the rooftop. "Our stonemason's mark. One hundred and forty-eight candles, too. That's one candle for each year that I have searched for him. Well, not including the few hours we were together in the box last spring, after I found him

110

in New York. They don't really count, since we were separated so soon afterward. And right here, in this very store..."

Katherine had tried not to remind Ambergine of that fact. She almost hoped the gargoyle hadn't recognized Cassandra and Candles By Daye at all. But she had.

The little gargoyle broke down and cried again. It took a long time for Katherine to calm her down enough to get her into the yellow canvas backpack, and into the back of the van.

One hundred and forty-eight years. Katherine couldn't imagine looking for someone for that long. That would be more than two lifetimes. That would mean that when Ambergine had started looking for Gargoth, there were still slaves in America. There was no such thing as electric lightbulbs. No one had ever seen a movie or heard the radio or used a telephone.

It was a long time to miss someone.

Soon Cassandra, Katherine and Ambergine were on the road, heading out of Toronto and south toward New York City.

Before they got on the highway, Cassandra stopped the van and bought street vendor hot dogs (a veggie dog for herself) since it would be some time before they had a chance to eat again. For the first little while, the inside of the van was silent as they ate their hot dogs.

Even Ambergine tried one (she was unusually curious about what hot dog tasted like) but immediately spat it out and said she'd prefer to stick to apples. She took a crabapple out of her pouch and ate that.

Katherine found that interesting. Gargoth kept tobacco

in his pouch. Ambergine kept apples. She asked the little gargoyle about this.

"I always have a few apples and a water jug in my pouch. I never liked tobacco, anyway." Ambergine curled up her nose.

It was a long, dark, boring drive, so there's no point in telling you too much about it. Only three remotely interesting things happened.

The first thing occurred just outside of Toronto, on the highway. Cassandra's cell phone rang, and Katherine had to dig in her huge bag to find it. On the seventh ring, she found it and snapped it open…

"Hello?"

"Katherine!" Her mother's voice sounded very far away. "Katherine? Is that you! It's Mom! Where are you? What's going on? What do you mean you're driving to find Gargoth? What's happened?" In the background, Katherine could hear loud party music.

Katherine looked at Cassandra. "It's my mom," she whispered.

"You better talk to her," Cassandra said. "I'm driving. Let her know I'll call her as soon as I can stop safely in a few minutes."

Katherine took a deep breath and said, "Mom, Mom! It's okay. Yes, we're driving to find Gargoth. No, we don't know where he is, exactly. Well, a man stole him. Yes, stole him. We know who he is, and Ambergine knows where he lives. Ambergine. She's a gargoyle. Yes, she's here. She found Cassandra's rooftop. Just after Gargoth vanished. Yes, it's kind of a long story. Okay, I'll start at the beginning…"

That was a very long conversation, but eventually Katherine was able to convince her mother and father that she and Cassandra and Ambergine had everything under control. She agreed to phone every hour on the hour after that (which turned out to be rather annoying but helped calm her mother down). Her parents were going to leave the wedding to take the next flight back to Toronto, but that wasn't going to help them very much on the road to New York. Still, it was reassuring to know that as soon as her parents were back in Toronto, they would be following in their own car.

The second interesting happening came in the darkest hours of night and was rather sad. Ambergine was fast asleep.

When Katherine heard her snoring gently, she turned to Cassandra and spoke quietly. "Cassie, do you think we are actually going to find the man in the white straw hat?"

Cassandra hesitated. "I don't see why we wouldn't be able to find him. Ambergine seems fairly sure that she knows how to find the mansion again. We'll have to trust her."

Katherine bit her lip and said, "But what if he hurts Gargoth? For running away? Or what if he hides him somewhere so that we can't ever find him?" She couldn't help it; she started crying. "What if we never see him again?" She was sobbing now.

Cassandra put her hand on Katherine's arm. "We're not going to think like that, Katherine. Not yet. We have to believe we'll find him." She nodded toward the yellow canvas backpack. "Ambergine hasn't given up looking for almost a hundred and fifty years. I think we can look for him for a few more days…"

At that moment Ambergine woke up with a sigh. "Where are we?" she asked sleepily as she climbed out of the backpack.

"Not too far now, another few hours," Katherine answered back, handing her a map and pointing out where they were on the snaking highway.

Katherine watched the little gargoyle as she carefully looked at the map and cleared her throat. "Ambergine, there's something that I've been wanting to ask you…"

"Yes?" Ambergine answered without looking up.

"Well, Gargoth has told us all about his early life, and how he found his friend Philip, and how he found you. Well, I guess really you found him. And then how the two of you lived in a little French village for years, then in Paris and that you were somehow separated at Notre Dame." Katherine hesitated, because she really didn't want to say the next part, but she finished quickly. "And I know that you were separated again in Cassandra's store last year. But, well, I'm just wondering how you found him at all? I mean, how on earth did you find him in New York City? It's so big, and you looked for so long…and how did you help him escape the place he was in?" Katherine looked at Ambergine with huge eyes, begging her to tell the final piece of the story.

The gargoyle was thoughtful. "It's kind of dull, Katherine. I just kept looking, that's all there is to it. Not very strange or interesting, I'm afraid. But all right, if you want to know what happened in New York City, I'll tell you."

Ambergine's story was the third interesting thing to happen on that long journey. She made herself comfortable in the back seat of the little van as it sped along the highway and shared the final chapter of Gargoth's story with his old friends and her new ones.

Gargoth's Story, Last Year
The Great Reunion

Ambergine stepped out of her hiding place and shook her wings to wake herself up. It was a beautiful spring night, and the air was clear and warm.

She was looking toward New York City from the top of the city's largest cathedral. She stayed here from time to time, since it was a peaceful green place in the huge city, and because it reminded her of her home in Paris, so long ago.

She was perched between two statues of a small dog and a donkey, both a warm golden colour as the sun set in the west. It was almost time for her to begin her night-time search.

As long as she had lived among the stone gargoyles of New York, she had never really liked them. They were odd and difficult, nothing like the graceful stone statues of her days in Paris with Gargoth. They were strangely dressed people, or dogs (too many dogs, she thought, rolling her eyes), or fat, comical-looking animals from distant parts of the world.

But like every other place she had ever been, none of the gargoyles of New York was alive, like her.

Or Gargoth, wherever he was.

She drummed her claws against the stone turret and looked out over the city. In the distance, she could see busy people rushing home in cars, taxis, buses and trains. Millions of cars. Millions of people. She was glad she was too far from the city to hear much of the noise from it. She'd been there too long to really notice much of the goings-on in it, anyway.

Ambergine had been there long enough to see horse-drawn carriages give way to cars, gas street lamps turn into electric lights, and the streets fill with more than eight million people from all over the world.

She waddled to the edge of the turret and leaned against the pedestal of an enormous angel. She had lived among many angels, but none had answered her prayer, at least not yet. She ate an apple to give her some energy for the long night ahead then lifted her weary wings to the skies.

As she flew, night after night, searching and searching, she would let her mind wander.

This night she was thinking about the last time she had seen Gargoth on that terrible night in Paris. She had carefully followed the thieves and discovered they were going to somewhere called "New York" on something called a "ship" across something else called an "ocean". She smiled despite herself. That took some courage, finding out that a "ship" was a tiny piece of wood crossing an "ocean", which turned out to be an impossible amount of water. She didn't even want to think about how wretched she was as she hid away on that terrible ship so long ago, drenched with salty water which stung her poor wings, and no sunlight or apples to eat or water to drink.

And no Gargoth.

New York she understood. It was a great city, much like Paris, only angrier and louder somehow, with more huge buildings and people moving by quickly on the dirty streets below.

As she was thinking of this, she adjusted her flight to climb a dark road, through a large forest which wound up a hillside. New York City was falling behind her. She was going to search a new neighbourhood with huge homes, with statues and fountains in the rolling gardens behind them.

Ambergine found it odd that humans were so interested in statues and gargoyles. During her many years of searching, she'd had no problem finding yards filled with angels and cherubs and statues of all kinds.

But of course, it hadn't made any difference where she looked. Not so far, anyway.

She was flying just above the treetops. It was quiet, and very still. She decided it must be about two o'clock in the morning. Suddenly a huge mansion loomed out of the dark ahead of her, with a gigantic garden *full* of statues. She could see them glowing and pale in the moonlight.

It was too dark to see anything very clearly, so she took a moment to land on the wall near the garden and rest before going further. She took an apple from her pouch and ate it slowly as she looked over the huge garden. Her eyes slowly passed over the statues near her, when two things happened.

The first thing was she realized that the statue in

front of her was an *exact* replica of Gargoth, carrying a fishing rod. Another figure of Gargoth holding an apple was chained to its side.

The second thing was that the chained statue took a bite of its apple.

It wasn't a statue! *It was Gargoth himself!*

Ambergine squeaked. Her voice was gone. She spat her own apple out of her mouth and spluttered, trying to speak, but nothing would come out. She fell off the garden wall and rolled into the grass, helpless.

Her wings failed her. Her voice failed her. She found she was sobbing, lying foolishly in the grass.

But Gargoth had seen her fall from the wall and turned toward her, straining at his thick chain. "Who are you? Who is there?" his growly voice called.

She was at his side in a second, hugging him with all her might. It took only a moment for her to fly to the top of the next statue and release him from his heavy length of chain.

In a second he was free.

They fell and stumbled and cried. They joined their claws together and skipped and whooped, breathless, across the huge walled garden. Gargoth howled at the moon and picked up rocks and threw them as hard as he could at nearby statues, breaking off many stone noses and wingtips. Both gargoyles crowed and laughed, giddy, like little children.

Beside a pool with a gigantic statue of a Greek god, Gargoth and Ambergine danced and danced, splashing in the water as moonlight sparkled off the shimmering pool, gracing them with shadow and light.

But suddenly Gargoth froze. A second later, one of the mansion windows flew open, and a man with a white hat and thick glasses thrust his head out.

"What are you doing? Where are you?" came a loud, ugly voice.

Before she understood what had happened, Gargoth shoved Ambergine to the ground behind an angel statue, and whispered, "Shhhh. Be still!" his voice breaking with fear.

Ambergine looked into Gargoth's terrified face and up at the face of the man in the window.

She snarled, and her ears flattened against her head. She was reunited with the only thing that mattered to her in the entire world, and she was *not* going to let anything happen to him, ever again.

One thing that Ambergine was really good at was hiding. She'd made a career of it, hiding among humans in busy cities for hundreds of years. So she did the one thing that made sense; she grabbed Gargoth by the claw, and together they hid in that gigantic walled garden of stone and grass and water.

And no one was going to find them.

Gargoth's Story, Last Year
T-O-R-O-N-T-O

Ambergine and Gargoth crept silently away from the statue of the Greek god, skirting the nearby statues, and moving as quickly as they could. They waddled and ran, Ambergine in the lead, urging Gargoth along.

The man in the white straw hat slammed the window shut and vanished, but they knew he was coming. He would soon be out on the grounds among the statues, trying to find them.

"Where should we go?" Ambergine gasped frantically. Gargoth seemed unable to answer her.

She shook him and looked into his face. "Where? Gargoth, quickly! Where should we hide?"

But he barely seemed to notice her. His eyes were suddenly sullen and clouded, and he would not look at her. She dragged him to the back of a giant rearing horse and rider statue, which blocked them completely from the mansion. She gained them a few moments' time.

"Gargoth! Look at me," she began. But he would not. Instead he stared at the dark grass. "We don't have much time. Gargoth, please!" she whispered. "You must tell me what's wrong? Why won't you run?"

He looked at her evenly. "You can't be real," he said.

"You simply cannot be here. It has been too long. One hundred and forty years, or more? I've lost count. I have been abandoned alone for too long to believe it is really you." He turned away from her. "I have finally gone mad. Or perhaps I've died at last." He squatted on his haunches and refused to move. Ambergine grew desperate.

"No! No, Gargoth. You cannot give up now! You *must* believe it's me!" She positioned herself directly in front of him and held his face next to hers. "You and I share the mark of the stonemason Tallus. I know your first human friend was a boy named Philip. I know you left your tiny English village with him to go to France. I know you loved Mozart, and you fed apples to beggar children, and I know…" she hesitated, "and I know you can't fly."

Gargoth snorted with disgust. "Well, you seem to know much about me. I suppose you are Ambergine, after all these years. But…"

He was interrupted by a low laugh. He spun around to see the man in the white straw hat standing in the grass behind him.

"So, you have a friend, do you? How nice of her to drop in!" the man said.

Gargoth shook with fear, but Ambergine was already tugging at him, urging him to run. The gargoyles turned and fled, moving as quickly as they could along the dark grass. They darted behind statue after statue as the man stumbled after them. They hid and ran off in a different direction each time he fumbled past them in the dark. Despite his thick glasses, he really did not see very well at all.

Once the man came upon them, but they both froze

122

so still that he didn't see them. He saw only statues.

Another time he found their hiding spot and reached down to grab Gargoth, but Ambergine flew up in his face and spread her wings, screaming. He was so surprised that he jumped back, and Gargoth escaped.

All that long night, the two gargoyles eluded the man in the straw hat, again and again, in an endless game of cat-and-mouse through the huge walled garden. It was an exhausting, terrifying chase, and by dawn Ambergine wasn't sure how much longer she could run.

As morning came, they were hiding beside a long, low building. They were weary and nearly out of places to hide. The man was once again slowly working his way toward them, looking behind each statue then creeping along to the next.

It was made worse by the fact that he was teasing Gargoth as he crept along. "Gargoth, you know you can't escape me! You'll never really get away from me! Why even try?" he yelled. Gargoth scowled but stayed silent.

Just then a delivery truck pulled up to the door of the building near them and beeped its horn. A man in a work suit came out and waved the truck inside.

"Come on!" whispered Ambergine, pulling Gargoth along. They scurried into the building, just as the door shut with a clang behind them.

Gargoth was petrified. They were standing in a long, narrow hallway, stacked with boxes. The truck driver and the other man were loading the boxes into the back of the truck.

"*Shhh*. Quiet," Ambergine whispered. Just then, one of the men turned and saw the gargoyles hiding in the hall.

"Hey! What are these doing there?" The man trotted toward them. Ambergine was about to run, but Gargoth shook his head a fraction. There was no time to run and nowhere to go anyway. Both gargoyles froze as the man reached them and grabbed them roughly.

"Look! What should we do with these two? They must have fallen out of one of these boxes…"

The other man walked up and looked at the two gargoyles. He whistled and ran his hand over Gargoth's wings. "Wow. They look really real, don't they? The boss must be making them from something special." He looked at the two little gargoyles for a moment then at the stack of boxes beside him.

"I don't know where they came from, but just put them in one of these boxes. I'm already late. I've got to get going."

The first man shrugged and lifted the lid of the nearest box, carelessly tossing the two gargoyles inside. He resealed the lid and walked away.

Inside the box, Ambergine shuddered. They were surrounded by statues of Gargoth, packed in straw.

"What are these?" she whispered.

"Stolen images. Me. For years, decades, the man made statues that look just like me and sent them all over the world. All without my permission, of course."

"That's awful," was all she could think to say. Gargoth had a stony expression and looked too much like the cold, still statues in the box all around him. It frightened her.

"Why didn't you run away?" she asked, then immediately regretted it.

Gargoth's face turned into a stormy, angry grimace, his voice a low growl. "I tried many times, but as a boy he carried me in a cage everywhere he went. When he was a man, he would sometimes let me out, but he kept a very close eye on me. Or he kept me chained, as I was tonight."

Her eyes filled with tears, and she gently took Gargoth's claw in hers. She didn't know what to say, so she changed the subject.

"Where do you think we're going?" she whispered as quietly as she could.

"There's a word on the box, T-O-R-O-N-T-O. Do you know where that is?" Gargoth whispered back.

"No. I hope it's somewhere warm and sunny though," she replied, then fell silent. Just then the men lifted their box into the back of the truck.

"That's it for now," said the first man.

"Okay. See you next week," said the other.

With that, the truck pulled out of the building and drove away.

Chapter Twenty-Two
The River

As the sun rose over the horizon, Cassandra's little van sped into the outskirts of New York City, and immediately pulled into a twenty-four-hour rest stop off the highway. There was a huge river in front of them, with the giant city on the other side. An enormous bridge spanned the river before them. It was morning now, and the roads were filled with commuters.

Cassandra got out of the van, stretched, and handed Katherine a map. "I'm going to get some breakfast for us. Maybe you should wake up Ambergine and get her to show you where we need to go on this map."

Katherine sat on a picnic bench near the van, poring over the map. The yellow canvas backpack was resting on the table next to her. It was a beautiful sunny morning. It was going to be a really hot day.

"So, where do you think we should start looking, Ambergine?" she asked. The little gargoyle was peering at the map through the holes in the backpack, but she wasn't much help.

"I'm really not sure. I can't see anything from in here, and that map doesn't make any sense to me. If I could just get out of here, and look around, I might be able to get my bearings a little. At least enough to give us the general direction…"

Katherine opened the bag and took Ambergine out. "Be still, look like a statue," she whispered.

The little gargoyle sat perfectly still in Katherine's arms, looking out at the grand view of the mighty Hudson River, the expanse of bridge and the view of New York City in the distance.

"Well?" Katherine asked. "Any ideas?"

Ambergine's dark eyes were wide with surprise. "Why didn't you tell me we were beside the river, Katherine?" she said. "The river will guide us."

Ambergine knew the river would take them to their lost friend and companion eventually, but she wasn't as sure as she seemed that she would be able to find him. Driving a van on a roadway wasn't the same as flying over treetops.

And even if they did find the dark mansion, she wasn't sure she wanted to tell Katherine and Cassandra what they would find there.

Chapter Twenty-Three
The Dark Mansion

The van crept along the dark, winding road, high above the city. They had been driving much of the day, following the banks of the Hudson River. They had only stopped once, for lunch. It was late evening now, and Katherine and Cassandra were tired, grumpy and a little short-tempered.

Katherine was hanging out the window, holding a flashlight and looking up into the trees.

"I can't see her, slow down!" she said to Cassandra in the driver's seat.

The van slowed, and Katherine shone her flashlight into the trees. "We've lost her again. Pull over." The van pulled off the road into a lookout spot.

Below them sprawled the vast city, rolling out to the ocean in the distance. Millions of lights blazed from thousands and thousands upon thousands of buildings, factories and houses. They were too far away to hear anything, but the city was alive. New York was the city that never slept.

Katherine was too tired to notice. She got out of the van and stood waiting, looking up into the trees.

Within a few minutes, they heard a crashing from the treetops, then Ambergine appeared in the road beside her, looking tired and weary. All day she had given good enough directions on how to find the right road from inside the van, but now it was night-time, she could no longer see the road well enough. Instead, they had to follow her as she flew ahead of them in the treetops.

"It's this way, I think," Ambergine said and flew off again.

Katherine yelled after her, "Hey, shouldn't you take a break? Have something to drink? Maybe eat a little?" but the gargoyle didn't hear her. She was off into the treetops, continuing her search.

"I know I could use a break," Katherine grumbled, then sighed and climbed wearily back into the van, pointing out the new direction to Cassandra. "She went that way."

It wasn't easy following a small, lumbering gargoyle as she led the way up a hilly road. It was made even more difficult by Cassandra's driving, which wasn't great. She'd had only a very short nap that morning and was clearly very tired. The van lurched and jumped and staggered up the dark road, with Katherine hanging dangerously out the window, peering up into the trees.

Every once in a while, Ambergine would appear hovering in the road ahead of them and point them down a different turnoff, then she would disappear again into the treetops.

Occasionally they would lose sight of the gargoyle altogether and would have to wait beside the road until she doubled back and found them. It was tedious, tiring work for Cassandra and Katherine in the van, and even more tiring for Ambergine, who had flown for hours. She was nearing exhaustion.

Even worse, now and then a "helpful" local would notice that they were driving very slowly and looking lost (although it was a little odd that they were looking up into the trees to find their way) and would stop to offer them assistance. Katherine and Cassandra had to pretend that they were French-Canadian and didn't speak any English to get rid of one particularly nosy person.

But as it got darker and the winding road took them further and further from the city, there were fewer and fewer cars passing by them, then fewer and fewer houses altogether.

Eventually, by midnight, it was pitch black, and the occupants of the little van were completely alone, high above the city on a dark, dangerous road.

They had lost sight of Ambergine once again, for the longest time so far. Katherine was straining out the window looking up, when…BANG!

She and Cassandra both jumped. Katherine banged her head on the window frame.

"OUCH!"

"What the…" Cassandra slammed on the brakes and pulled the van over to the side of the road. Katherine got out.

Ambergine was sitting on the top of the van, exhausted and with a very frightened look on her face. "Sorry," she said, "I didn't mean to land so hard. I've found it. I've found the dark mansion. It's about five minutes ahead on the right. It's pitch black, though, so

I don't think anyone is home. It looks abandoned and empty…" Her voice grew very quiet.

Katherine and Ambergine looked at each other. What if no one *was* home? What if he wasn't there?

Katherine called inside the van, "It's okay! It's Ambergine. She's found the dark mansion. We're almost there…"

For the next half hour, the three friends sat outside in the hot night air, talking and thinking up a plan.

How were they going to get inside the dark mansion? How were they going to grab Gargoth, if and when they found him?

And how were they going to convince the man in the white straw hat to let them take him with them?

It was going to take something sneaky and tricky and likely a little dangerous. And probably quite brave.

Ambergine, who had flown for decades and decades and decades in search of Gargoth, who never gave up and who certainly wasn't about to give up now, would be brave enough for them all.

Chapter Twenty-Four
Statues in the Night

The van was parked off in the darkness, just out of sight of the dark mansion. Cassandra and Katherine had searched through the boxes in the back of the van and come up with some strange looking clothes; Cassandra was wearing a big floppy felt hat, tiny owlish reading glasses and a large, brightly-coloured Hawaiian shirt hanging over her long flowery skirt. She looked like a giant flowering plant.

They were really hoping that she looked like a lost tourist, or at least nothing like Cassandra Daye. Her height was a problem though. She found an old cane in the back of the van and hunched over it, hoping not to look so tall. She was going to pretend to be a lost French-Canadian tourist, separated from her tour bus, which seemed unlikely, but it was the best plan they could come up with.

Katherine was using black makeup from an old makeup kit she found in the van, covering her cheeks and nose. She looked like a commando on a night raid.

Which is, in fact, what she was.

Ambergine was waiting in the woods beside the wall

of the garden when Cassandra and Katherine joined her. Ambergine shot a strange look at Cassandra, but said only, "Good. Tell her she looks really…different. Perhaps he won't know who she is."

"Everyone know what happens next?" Katherine asked. They all nodded.

"Okay, here goes. Good luck," said Cassandra. She hugged Katherine, shook Ambergine's claw, then toddled off past the huge gates and up the dark, strange driveway to knock on the door of Gargoth's greatest enemy.

Katherine watched as Cassandra, the only bit of colour and light against the backdrop of the enormous, scary mansion, moved slowly away down the driveway toward the gigantic front door. She felt a sudden pang of fear. What were they getting themselves into?

As Cassandra disappeared into the gloom, Katherine and Ambergine slipped quietly over the wall of the huge garden and began to creep slowly along behind the bushes and trees and statues to the back of the enormous house.

And what a bizarre house it was. It stood at the edge of the valley, looking down across the vast plain toward New York City in the distance. It had colossal windows, a towering chimney, and slanted rooftops with ivy climbing up every wall. On every corner of the house and covering almost every inch of grass was a giant statue, of a goddess, or a lion, or a horse or a gryphon.

Or a gargoyle.

There were gargoyles *everywhere*, thousands of them. And every single one of them looked exactly like Gargoth.

Katherine was kneeling at the bottom of a statue of Gargoth rowing a boat.

"How strange. He's everywhere, but we don't know where he is. This is really weird," she whispered to Ambergine. She was creeping along the damp grass behind Ambergine, who was hovering just above the ground. They were moving quietly from statue to statue, staying hidden from view.

The next statue was of Gargoth playing tennis. The one after that was of him playing a guitar. And still another was of him wearing a straw hat with a long piece of grass in his teeth, painting a fence.

And on and on it went. They all looked just like Gargoth, but none of them was doing anything that Gargoth would do. Not the Gargoth she knew, anyway.

Poor Gargoth, she thought. *I'm starting to see why he was so upset about this place… It's really creepy…*

Just then Katherine crept past a length of thick, heavy chain hanging from a statue of Gargoth with a fishing rod. She winced and drew in her breath: this was where the man in the white straw hat kept Gargoth chained. It was like a house of horrors.

As they crept along, Katherine saw a group of long, low buildings at the edge of the forest. She could barely make them out in the gloom. There was something disturbing and dark about them.

"Ambergine, is that the building you and Gargoth escaped from?" she whispered.

Ambergine didn't even look. "Yes, that's it. That's a night I'd like to forget. There was a *lot* of screaming going on."

"Who was screaming?"

"The man in the white straw hat. Just as we were driving off in the back of the truck, we could hear him screaming, 'Where is he? Where is he?' Luckily the truck driver didn't hear him, since he was wearing those music things in his ears, and kept going. But the man in the white straw hat knew where the truck was headed." Ambergine shuddered. She shook her head as though to clear the memory.

They began creeping along from statue to statue again, slowly making their way to the back of the mansion. Katherine tried not to glance over at the low, dark buildings in the distance. She couldn't help it; they made her shudder.

After a while, Ambergine stopped and motioned to her to sit behind a huge statue of an angel. It hid them completely from the windows of the house.

"Wait here," the gargoyle whispered. "This spot is safe for now… I'm going for a closer look, but you can't come…"

She flew carefully toward the back of the mansion, hovering over a large, dark pool of water with a giant statue of a Greek god in the middle. It was Triton, with a huge, slippery-looking merman tail and a three-pronged Trident in his hand. She was hovering near his tail, looking in the window of a green sitting room.

Meanwhile, Cassandra had made it to the front door. She took a deep breath then pulled the enormous chain. A distant BONG rang out inside the mansion.

Nothing happened.

She pulled it again, harder this time.

Another deep BONGGGG rang out, but still no one came to the door.

Cassandra scratched her nose and looked around. She shrugged. "I guess I'll have a seat," she said to herself.

There were two garden seats off to one side of the front door. Cassandra was just about to lower herself into one of them when the front door suddenly opened. She jumped to her feet.

The man in the white straw hat was standing there, his thick glasses reflecting the rising moon. "Cassandra Daye. How lovely that you could come to my little home on the mountain. I am The Collector. Please come in," he said.

The Collector? What kind of a name is that?

She looked at him, then stepped inside. "So much for the disguise," she thought as she crossed the dark threshold. What else could she do?

Chapter Twenty-Five
The End and the Beginning

Cassandra followed the Collector into the dark hallway. There was no light at all. It was almost pitch black.

"How can he see anything, with no lights on *and* wearing such thick glasses?" she thought.

Cassandra had the sense that there were creatures all through the gigantic house, but as she got closer to the "animals", she realized they were statues, hundreds of them. As she walked past each one, a different face jumped out of the darkness at her. An elephant. A leopard. A goddess. An angel. A satyr.

And in the centre of the hallway was the largest statue of all: a gigantic Gargoth, with his pipe clenched in his teeth. He was easily ten metres tall, his wingtips just brushing the ceiling of the cavernous, creepy hallway.

"So, as you can see, I have quite a large collection," the man was saying. "I collect beautiful statues, and interesting…specimens."

Cassandra shot back, "Even if they are alive? Even if they're not yours to collect?"

The Collector smiled. "Yes, yes, Ms Daye, I thought you'd say that. I know your love of statues and…beings like the one you search for. I've watched you and your friends for months, The little female gargoyle was most helpful there. She's a very persistent creature. Do you know, she's never stopped looking for the other one? It's been over one hundred years."

"For one hundred and forty-eight years, actually," Cassandra said, with a hint of pride in her voice.

"Anyway," he continued, ignoring her, "she led me right to you. And to your friend, the young Newberry person…the girl from the soccer game, the one staying at your store…." Here he shook his head and tut-tutted. "Most unfortunate that she had to get involved… Where is she, anyway? I'm sure she's around here somewhere…"

"I don't know who you're talking about," Cassandra shot back. But she was suddenly very nervous about her decision to bring Katherine to this place. This man was dark and dangerous, and clearly obsessed with Gargoth. People who are obsessed are often very reckless, and they don't care who they hurt to get what they want.

The Collector lead Cassandra into a green room looking out over a dark pool with a huge statue of a Greek god in it, its merman tail silvery in the moonlight. Beyond it, she could vaguely see the vast garden through the gloom, filled with hundreds of pale, shadowy statues.

Cassandra spoke. "Okay. So you know who I am. That's fine. I know who you are, too. You stole my friend Gargoth, and I'm here to get him back. Where is he?"

The Collector smiled darkly. "Oh, he's quite safe. He's the most valuable piece in my entire…collection. There's nothing else like him anywhere in the world.

Except for that little gargoyle right there. And as luck would have it, you've brought her right to me." He pointed out the window toward the statue in the pool. At that moment, Cassandra saw Ambergine hovering above the water, looking stricken. She shot out of sight above the window as quickly as she could. But it was too late, the vile man had seen her.

But he did not see Cassandra Daye as she stood behind him. Her cane quite mysteriously (and expertly) jabbed into a huge statue of a dancing dog. She was quite clumsy that way.

Several things happened at once.

The dancing dog statue tottered then fell with a great smash into the windows of the sitting room, but not before it banged into several other statues on the way.

As the dancing dog statue fell, it hit another statue, which hit another, then another. It was a domino cascade of statues! For a few moments, Cassandra could see nothing but slowly tottering statues as they fell banging into each other, crashing with gigantic thuds to the marble floor. As the dust rose, Cassandra heard a shout and saw the Collector entangled in the arms of a falling angel, slowly pinning him to the ground as it fell.

Katherine, who had seen it all happen from just outside the broken window, yelled into the room, "Hurry, Cassandra! Out here!"

Cassandra climbed through the window into the hot damp night air, just as they both heard a shout from the rooftop. "Up here! UP HERE! HURRY!"

It was Ambergine.

They needed to get to the roof somehow. Katherine looked around. Her eyes fell on the Greek god, whose trident rose thirty metres into the air, just short of the roof.

"Come on!" she cried.

They ran to the statue. "Climb, Cassandra!" Katherine yelled. The two clambered up the side of the Greek god. Cassandra was surprisingly graceful as she scampered up the god's scaly tail and slippery body. There were plenty of footholds and handholds to grasp, and once or twice she could have sworn that the statue itself helped her along, although she couldn't be completely sure.

Just as she was about to reach the roof, Cassandra heard stirring beneath her. Someone was moving in the green sitting room below them.

"Hurry! Climb, Katherine!" she gasped.

They struggled their way to the roof, using the ancient ivy as a ladder for the last few metres to the rooftop.

But they made it. And across the roof was Ambergine, waving at them frantically to hurry.

She had found Gargoth.

He was trapped in a cage, hanging from the end of a long pole sticking out over the edge of the rooftop. He was dangling over the valley with nothing but empty air beneath him. There was another cage beside him, hanging open and empty.

He was shivering and frightened and utterly desperate. "Don't come any closer, I beg you," he called. "Please. My friends, I have caused you enough trouble. You don't know, he will be here…you must flee…" Gargoth's voice was full of despair.

"We came for you, Gargoth. We would always come for you," Katherine shouted back. She wanted nothing more than to climb out onto the pole and hug him, to save him and take him home. "We'll get you out of there somehow…"

Ambergine was slowly edging out to the end of the pole. Katherine and Cassandra stood impatiently at the edge of the roof.

"Hurry, Ambergine!" Cassandra urged, banging her hands on the wall.

"I wonder why there are two cages? What's the empty one for?" Katherine asked.

A voice spoke. "Why, it's for her, of course." The Collector stood on the rooftop a few metres away.

Katherine gasped. Cassandra spun around to look at him. He was covered in statue dust, his white straw hat battered and squashed, his thick glasses askew.

"It's perfect. I knew she'd come, if I just laid the bait. Now I have them both. For all time." He was tossing something large and shiny up and down in his hand. It was the key to Gargoth's cage.

"What makes you think we'll let you have them?" Cassandra answered, angry now. She drew herself up to her full height and turned on him with real menace in her voice. Despite the fact that she looked like a crazy giant flower, the Collector drew back a step.

"We'd never leave them here with you. They're not yours. They…they…they belong to each other, not to anyone else," she finally said.

"Oh, I think you'll let me keep them. Or I just toss this key away forever." As he said this, the Collector dangled the key over the edge of the rooftop.

"Which will it be?" he asked, with a terrible grimace on his ugly face.

"You're a monster!" cried Katherine. She tried to jump at him, but he dodged her with a wicked laugh and moved further down the rooftop, still holding the key over the edge. He was surprisingly nimble.

No one had noticed that Ambergine had made it to the end of the pole and was passing something through the bars to Gargoth.

ZING! ZING!

In a second, two well-thrown crabapples hit the Collector hard, right between the eyes. He was so surprised, he dropped the key. Katherine was beside him in a flash, and kicked the little key over to Cassandra (a perfect soccer kick, too), who snatched it up and held it out as far as she could toward Ambergine. (It helped that she was so tall and that her arms were much longer than most people's).

Ambergine scrambled along the pole, grabbed the key, and had Gargoth's door open in a second. The cage swung dangerously.

The Collector ran to the pole. "NO! NO! You're mine!" he screamed, with his arms open. He was pulling at the pole, slowly dragging it toward him, while Gargoth's cage dangled and bounced at the end. The open cage door was swinging furiously, with the little gargoyle clinging to the bars inside.

Cassandra and Katherine tried to stop the Collector, and for a long while the three figures struggled together at the end of the pole. But the more they fought, the more Gargoth's cage bounced dangerously, and he was in grave danger of falling to his death. Cassandra and Katherine had to stop.

The friends stood, helpless. The pole slowly edged closer to the rooftop as Gargoth's greatest enemy dragged it toward him. Ambergine was flying in front of the swaying cage, holding Gargoth's claw, whispering something to him in urgent, low tones.

Gargoth looked back at the rooftop. He gulped. He was terrified and shook from head to toe as his cage drew closer to the man who had tormented him for so long.

But he was a brave gargoyle. There was no going back. He had waited several lifetimes for this very moment.

He drew a deep breath, then with a tremendous leap, he sprang from the cage into the night air, clasping Ambergine's claw in his.

A long howl of "NOOOO!" went out over the night, as the Collector leapt for the cage a second too late. His arms closed around the cage at the end of the pole, and he was left hanging there for dear life, suspended and dangling over the valley, where just moments before Gargoth had been.

Katherine and Cassandra watched, breathless, as both gargoyles tumbled down, down, down through the air, end over end over end. Ambergine's wings were beating hard and fast, and she kept them from falling too far as she clung to Gargoth's claw. She struggled and beat her wings as hard as she could, gasping for air. She could fly for both of them, but not for long.

Suddenly Katherine leaned over the edge of the rooftop

and yelled at the top of her lungs, "GARGOTH! TRY!" She couldn't see them, the pair had plunged so far into the darkness of the valley below, but she yelled anyway.

Cassandra joined in. From far below, just above the treetops and clutching Ambergine's claw, Gargoth heard them.

He looked at the treetops below him, then at the moonlight far above. He could faintly make out two cages dangling at the edge of a pole far above him, and the figure of a man clinging to one empty cage as it bounced and banged dangerously in the air.

Gargoth felt a sudden stab of anger. He knew two things for certain: he was *not* going back, and he would *not* be anyone's prisoner, ever again.

With a determined growl, he stretched his leathery wings and began to beat them, harder and harder. He was clumsy and frightened, and every wingbeat drew great rattling breaths of exertion from his small chest. But he didn't stop, and Ambergine didn't let him go, struggling as she was to keep them both aloft above the trees.

Then it happened. Slowly Gargoth felt the air move over his wings and saw the treetops below him begin to steady and fall away. He rose into the dark, too clumsy to turn back and thank his friends. But they saw him, caught against the moon, and a great cheer went up from the rooftop.

His heart beating fast, his long-unused wings shaky and weak, Gargoth took Ambergine's claw in his. Borne up at last, wing-tip to wing-tip, they flew off into the night, casting their shadow as one over the wide world below.

There are many adventures ahead of them, more than there are behind. They will travel to new places and encounter new friends (and I'm sad to say, foes as well). They will return again to T-O-R-O-N-T-O, to the candle-lit rooftop at Cassandra Daye's and to Katherine's welcoming backyard with Milly the cat.

But most important of all, you and I know that from now on in their long and eventful lives, nothing can part them ever again.

Wherever they go, they go together.

Epilogue

It is many years from now, a long time after our story ends.

One fine late summer day, a young boy is walking in an old English churchyard. It is a very pretty place, surrounded by rolling green hills and chestnut trees. A small, sweet river runs along beside the church courtyard. An ancient stone lion looks to the west, regal and golden, his left ear broken off and lying in the grass at his feet.

An old woman is walking nearby in the abandoned apple orchard, running her hands over the trunks of each tree as she walks by.

The boy is wondering what it would have been like to live in the village, so long ago. He is wondering what stories might have been told in the churchyard, and who would have lived here for centuries and centuries and eaten those apples.

Suddenly a rustling in the ivy catches his eye. He looks more closely, and for a moment he is sure he sees two little figures disappear behind the church tower. He sees the outline of a wing, a leathery head, and maybe a claw.

Stranger still, just as he is sure he imagined it, an apple core lands in the grass near him, followed by a trill of laughter. He picks it up and examines it, amazed.

"Grandmother Katherine," the boy shouts. "Someone threw this apple core at me! I think they were laughing…" Despite himself, he starts to smile.

His grandmother picks an apple and takes a bite, looking at him thoughtfully for a few moments. Then she turns and walks toward the church tower, calling over her shoulder, "Come with me. There are some friends I'd like you to meet!"

Philippa Dowding is an award-winning copywriter for magazines as varied as *Maclean's, Chatelaine, Today's Parent* and *Canada's History*. Her poetry has appeared in *Mother-Verse, The Adirondack Review, The Literary Review of Canada* and other journals.

The Gargoyle Overhead is her second children's book and is the sequel to *The Gargoyle in My Yard* (2009). She lives with her family in Toronto. Her website is
www.pdowding.com

A Note from the Author on the History in this Book

Gargoyles live a long time, which is why this book covers 400 years of fascinating history. Here are some of the true historical events mentioned in this story:

—1665   The Great Plague sweeps through England, killing at least 100,000 people
—1778   Mozart's Paris Symphony debuts in France
—1789-1799   The French Revolution kills thousands
—1939   The World's Fair in New York City introduces television and robotics

There are other historical touches here and there. For example, a "tinder-pistol" really was an early kind of lighter, and "Troll-my-Dame" is a very old marble game.

To learn more about historical times, search the internet or visit your local library!